Humph's War

WAYNE CLARK

Published by Wayne Clark YUL/NYC

ISBN: 978-1-0689709-0-0

Cover and book design: Nell Chitty

Also in the NY PI Series:

One Murder Too Many

Busted on Broadway

Artistic License

Other novels
by Wayne Clark:

he & She

That Woman

Hollywood via Orchard Street

Vinegar Hill Blues

wayne-clark.com

ACKNOWLEDGEMENTS

The author would like to thank Barry Clark and Anishella Jean-Baptiste for their encouragement and insightful assistance.

CONTENTS

CHAPTER 1	1
CHAPTER 2	7
CHAPTER 3	17
CHAPTER 4	25
CHAPTER 5	31
CHAPTER 6	35
CHAPTER 7	47
CHAPTER 8	53
CHAPTER 9	59
CHAPTER 10	69
CHAPTER 11	79
CHAPTER 12	85
CHAPTER 13	95
CHAPTER 14	103

CHAPTER 15   109

CHAPTER 16   111

CHAPTER 17   121

CHAPTER 18   131

CHAPTER 19   135

CHAPTER 20   141

CHAPTER 21   151

CHAPTER 22   153

CHAPTER 23   159

CHAPTER 24   167

CHAPTER 25   177

CHAPTER 26   183

CHAPTER 27   193

CHAPTER 28   203

CHAPTER 1

OUT of boredom on a miserable morning in May 1941, Humph attended a murder scene. He'd heard calls on the police radio directing cars to East 34th Street, just west of Third Avenue. When he arrived, he saw that his flamboyantly erratic, old Irish cop friend, Duffy, had beat him to it. He was at the wheel of a borrowed 1941 Chrysler Thunderbolt convertible. At first, Duffy said he'd been loaned the car by a friend. Further conversational investigation revealed that he'd "sort of borrowed" the sleek vehicle from a friend. And even more in-depth investigation revealed that it belonged to a gangster who had just been sent away for life for murder. Humph didn't want to know any more details.

Between him and Duffy, they knew four of the cops at the scene. The body was bloated by good living. Blood decorated his chest, from throat to belly button. The victim was Otto Schmidt, said one of the detectives. They hadn't the slightest information about why his time clock had been punched. They could only surmise: "It was likely a Murder Inc. job. Super effective, super clean crime scene."

Murder Inc., becoming the best-known Brooklyn company not on the stock exchange, was in the news a lot these days. To join, you had to be an assassin with an impeccable track record, notable skills, a yapper that stayed shut when needed and, by nature, unquestioning about assignments. Most often, targets were gangsters that the various mob families were annoyed by, or borrowers who failed to understand that loans were repayable on demand in the case of default. The mob liked Murder Inc—one-stop shopping. Annoyances disappeared with a nod or an index finger laid alongside a nose.

"How was Herr Schmidt mob-connected?" asked Humph. The blank looks reminded him of school on test day when students picked up their test papers and read the first question they had to answer.

It was far too early for Duffy and Humph to invade a tavern. They instead chose to go to his Bowery abode where they quickly resumed the conversation the police radio had interrupted an hour earlier.

Humph had arrived at Duffy's place full of frustrations. One was the fact he had no major case to investigate. But the biggest frustration, Duffy surmised, was the fact that the U.S. had not joined the war effort. For almost two years the papers had been full of horrid German aggressions throughout much of Europe—Poland, France, who'd be next? And England, how long before it was invaded?

"Everything else," said Humph, "in the face of all that, seems irrelevant, petty. Why as Americans don't we want to have anything to do with a war that will involve us whether we like it or not?"

A few minutes later, after sucking in the Scotch Duffy had poured him, he started to describe his morning as an example of how meaningless things had become in the face of the horrors of Europe.

"Duff, you know I adore Rebecca."

"As well you should. After all, she solved your last case." He knew that would irritate the big man.

Humph, from long experience, ignored him.

"But here I am looking at the headlines. In this morning's case, Yugoslavia was falling to the Nazis. Before I settle my eyes on the next war dispatch, the girls implore me to take advantage of some kind of damn sale they'd read about in the paper. In less than an hour, there I was in a hat store on Fifth Avenue."

The shop, in the 500 block of Fifth, was called "Knox the Hatter".

"Once there, while I grumbled, Eve handed me a clipping from the previous day's *New York Times*. She said she remembered well when I bellyached about ditching my ancient bowler for a fedora. That was probably a good ten years ago. It took a year or two, but I eventually agreed that it suited me. She had me there."

The clipping Eve held was an ad placed by the shop. It was announcing the "Knox Coronado $10, the hat with many personalities." The shop promised to adapt it to the buyer's personality, adding that it takes eight different creases. They promised to fit the buyer exactly. The title of the ad was: "YOU'RE SURE TO PLEASE HER".

"After reading the clipping with the ad, I knew I was doomed to passing my day in irrelevance. Furthermore— and never, Duff, never mention this complaint to either Rebecca or Eve—I had given in to bullying women. They had kidnapped my day. My only out was to please, as the ad promised, 'her' and 'her'."

Duffy raised his glass, understanding his friend entirely.

"Under duress, extreme female duress," Humph said, "I would purchase this Coronado thing." Upon leaving the store, he handed the hat to Rebecca to carry. "Be careful," he said to her. "You're going to trip over that victory smile."

"I'm just happy we had a fun day shopping," she said.

"No," Humph corrected. "You're gloating. And so are you, Eve."

"I had lost," he said to Duffy. He then described the rest of the day.

He said the girls were still bubbly when they arrived at Third Avenue and stood waiting for the M101 bus. It had only recently replaced the old streetcar service.

The two-tone dark green and cream-colored bus arrived minutes later. Once seated near the back, Rebecca grabbed Humph's hat and handed him the Coronado.

"Put it on. You'll be the handsomest man on the bus." Humph, realizing they were near the back of the bus, figured no one would see him in the hat.

When they got home to Tompkins Square, the girls descended on him, Eve offering a Scotch first. "Here you go, Grumpy Gus. What's eating you?"

The answer came faster than she had expected.

"Boredom!"

Rebecca knew he meant not having any cases to solve. "Shopping doesn't fill the void," he said pointedly.

Rebecca had stolen his thunder in the last big case, solving the robbery at the Met. He was happy to be in the back seat while his wife piled up the accolades she deserved.

Like Eve, she had Broadway to fall back on now that her police shield sat on the bedroom nightstand. It rested atop a commendation from the NYPD commissioner. It sat there like a Christmas card she needed to thank someone for. Ego was not an issue with Rebecca, living a full life was.

Despite the gloom and horror abroad, the lights on Broadway shone bright. The one show that attracted Humph was Lillian Hellman's *Watch on the Rhine*, about a German-born anti-fascist who returns to the United States with his American-born wife and daughter, only to find himself torn between his loyalty to his family and his duty to fight against the Nazis.

America was interested in the war, but so far only from afar.

Rebecca had done her usual magic in her designs for Hellman's play. She had more energy than Humph ever possessed. As for Eve, she landed a replacement role in *The Man Who Came to Dinner*. Although it premiered two years earlier, this comedy by George S. Kaufman and Moss Hart continued to sell tickets. Before landing the role, Eve was starting to think age was about to sweep her off the stage. The rehearsal work had become too demanding. Her part in *The Man Who* was a speaking role.

"I'm still on Broadway!" she exclaimed when she landed the role.

Humph had no such great news. Several times a week he walked to the old precinct to see Chief Detective Higgins, but he left empty-handed. Most of the cases Higgins mentioned were profoundly solvable by the NYPD's own detectives. Humph wanted to be challenged. After the visit, he went to the neighborhood cop bar that once served as an exclusive cop speakeasy. Many beers into the evening, a couple of cops began surmising that there probably were Nazi spies in New York.

"That was when I decided to see you, Duffy. I came to find out what rumors you might have been hearing of late."

"To be honest, I haven't given it a moment's thought. Maybe because I was born in the old country. It's a small world on the other side of the ocean. Tiny, puffed-up little countries all over the place. They've been tripping over each other forever. There are democrats, communists, socialists, fascists and just plain idiots who've been living cheek by jowl for centuries. Here, we can't even tolerate anyone who isn't a Democrat or a Republican."

Humph didn't think Duffy's case was entirely valid. He reminded the Irishman that he was born and bred on the Lower East Side where the squalor was a cosmopolitan as anywhere in the world.

"The difference," said Duffy, "is that your neighbors didn't have guns and bombs and planes to decide disputes about a rent increase or a hike in the price of apples."

Humph stared at him for a moment.

"You know, Duffy, you're right."

"It's always the rich who start wars, the ones who can afford them. Poor people, the average American, can't afford wars. I'd chose the battles on the LES any day."

Duffy then offered Humph a refill.

"Time to get real, Humph. I know you. You're dreaming of going off to fight for freedom, for us or any damned country desperate enough to accept you. You're too old, my friend."

That hurt. When Humph stopped thinking of his friend's words later that evening, he had to accept the truth.

Rebecca was late coming home, which wasn't unusual. On the way home, he bought a copy of the *New York Word-Telegram*. For a change, war news didn't sit atop the day's happenings. Instead there was another one of those technological progress stories he couldn't keep up with. According to the story, New York now had television stations, two of them. They had just signed on the air for the first time. The first was WNBT Channel 1 and the second was WCBW Channel 2.

"Are you going to buy me an antenna for my birthday?" Rebecca said later that evening.

"And, I suppose, you would like a TV to go with that?"

"You've got time," said Rebecca. "The story says both stations will begin broadcasting on July 1, more than a month away."

CHAPTER 2

THE next day's papers merely reported that a German-American had been gunned down, and police admitted they had no idea why. That was the man Humph and Duffy had seen the day before. The deceased apparently was an instructor at some kind of German-American school on Long Island.

Although Humph felt freed from his funk after the discussion with the Irishman, and later having passed a normal couple's evening with Rebecca, he also felt the gears grinding again when he read that news. The PI was in bull-mood. He had no evidence of anything, but that only meant there were a million possibilities. Rebecca always said such odds were depressing. Humph would just smile. "We'll see."

A new case, or at least a possible case, energized his step.

Humph made a B-line to Park Row to see his friend, Graham, the managing editor of the *New York World-Telegram*. Graham's knowledge of news events was encyclopedic.

He had one question. What was this German-American school on Long Island?

For some reason, Graham had the answer at his fingertips.

"It was called Camp Siegfried. The fact that it even existed boggles the mind."

Humph interrupted. "You said existed, past tense. Has it closed?"

"Not yet," said Graham, "but I think the New York Secretary of State is going to come down hard on the camp in the near future. It might even become a federal case because there are other such camps. I know there's one in New Jersey and another in Pennsylvania, and there are probably more in the rest of the country."

"So, what is this camp exactly?" Humph asked.

Graham held up his hand and called over a copy boy. He asked the lad to run to the paper's morgue and get the file on Camp Siegfried.

While waiting for the file, Graham outlined the basics. The camp was supposedly created as a summer camp for kids, exclusively for kids of German-American parents. "It was set up by an organization you might have heard of, the German American Bund, an organization that aims to spread Nazi ideology within the United States.

"Like you, Humph, I hadn't heard of it until fairly recently. I was amazed that this summer camp has been operating for five years now. Thousands and thousands of German-Yankee kids and their parents spend their summers there near a Long Island hamlet I'd never heard of, some place called Yaphank, Long Island."

The office boy reappeared with two file folders of news clippings and photographs.

Before leaving, the boy spoke to Graham.

"I'm going on the lunch run soon, sir. What would you like?"

"Tuna salad sandwich with a dash of pepper."

Graham handed him some cash, and the boy took off.

Turning one of the folders around so Humph and Duffy could read the contents, Graham, reading from one of the clippings, said:

"Yeah, tens of thousands of people attend the camp for summer fun. You know, swimming, sailing, hiking. However, they spend much of their day being indoctrinated with Nazi philosophy, if you can call racism and brutality a philosophy. However, the good Americans of Yaphank appear to need no indoctrination. Not only did they name a street after Hitler, but they also paid homage to two other Nazis by creating a Goebbels Street and a Goering Street."

"What in the name of all that's holy is wrong with Americans!" exclaimed Duffy. "Are they evil, too, or just plain ignorant of the world?"

"I suspect the latter," Graham said.

"I've got to see this for myself," Duffy said. "Can we enter the camp?"

Graham said there was nothing to stop them from going to the hamlet, but he doubted the Bund people would allow them unfettered access to the students.

The three men were silent for a while. The whole thing was hard to imagine happening on American soil.

Graham broke the silence.

"You speak some German, don't you Humph?"

"A little. My parents spoke it."

"Then you would probably fare better than your friend, the Irish ambassador to the United States."

Humph and Duffy stood up.

"But before you go," said Graham. He held out another clipping. Humph took it and read it. He then summarized it for Duffy. The essence was that the Bund used the camp to teach espionage methods to the young people. They also encouraged sexual promiscuity in the hope of increasing the population of indoctrinated young people. For a veteran newspaperman and two longtime cops and investigators to be astonished by the revelations about Camp Siegfried and the Bund itself said a lot.

Once outside, Humph and Duffy headed for Duffy's favorite pub. Under the circumstances, it was the only place to go. There was no need to discuss their destination.

The saloon was always full and always animated to the point of being deafening. No one could possibly overhear a stranger's conversation. It was so boisterous that Duffy had a theory that the noise made it impossible to sense whether you'd had too much to drink. Which, he said, was a good thing, or at least it was until the moment you decided to stand up to head home.

With neither man having a case to work on, they decided to go to Yaphank, Long Island, wherever that was, in the morning.

"That is, in the late morning," Duffy said by way of clarification.

When they met up the next day, Duffy asked Humph whether he knew how to get there. Humph said he did, which Duffy figured meant he didn't have to use his own brain quite yet. Humph led him to 34th Street and the magnificent Penn Station. They boarded a Long Island Railroad train for Long Island. Shockingly, knowing what they did about their destination, the train was called the Camp Siegfried Special. Sixty miles later they descended on Yaphank, quiet beyond belief for two Manhattanites—residential, almost rural.

Gazing about, Duffy said, "So, this is the West Hamptons. Heard about it but never been. Where's your yacht, Humph?"

The pair wandered until they found a local. Directions in hand, they discussed strategy. On the way, they encountered the infamous Hitler Street.

"If I were a city sanitation worker, Humph, I'd refuse to pick up garbage on this street." Humph clapped him on the back.

They decided Humph would do the talking once they encountered a possible Nazi. Humph had worked up a few phrases in German the night before. One of them was that, yes, he was born of German parents but had lost most of the language over the years. He stood before a mirror and repeated it until it sounded smooth and natural.

It was a beautiful day. Duffy asked, "You smell the sea?"

"I do indeed," answered Humph. "I bottled a jar of that smell. It's on my yacht if you ever want a whiff before we return to New York."

Duffy stared up at him until he realized Humph was pulling his leg.

They spotted a cab and flagged it down.

"Camp Siegfried," Humph told the driver in English but manufacturing a slight German accent.

It was a five-minute ride.

To their left was a wooden shack. It bore a large hand-painted sign that said "Willkommen". It was written in a way to look amateurish, friendly—child-friendly perhaps.

Humph and Duffy entered. Humph introduced himself as a German-American writer. He said he was fascinated that tens of thousands of New Yorkers of German descent visited the camp every year. He said he was a freelance writer and, until he investigated further, he would have no idea who might be a client for his story.

Duffy was profoundly impressed with how smoothly Humph lied.

With his German-accented accent in tack, he asked to interview some of the young people about their experiences at this exceptional camp. The woman behind the desk disappeared, with apologies, for about ten minutes. When she returned, she said, "Your request can be arranged, sir."

The first girl they interviewed was eighteen years old, glowing with youth. She loved the camp. This was her third year there. She added that she had found the most marvelous boyfriends there. She didn't even giggle after the admission.

The second girl was a different story. She was shy. She avoided eye contact. And her face was bruised.

Humph told her she didn't have to talk with him if she didn't want to. She replied that she was ordered to talk to him.

"Ordered?"

"Yes, sir. By the matron."

Humph and Duffy looked at each other for a second. Something didn't smell right.

"Miss," said Duffy, "what is your name?"

"Anke," she said.

"May I ask about that bruise?" asked Duffy in the same soft voice. "How did you get it?"

Anke didn't answer immediately.

Seconds later, Duffy, with his Irish lilt dialed up a notch, said, "I don't mean to intrude, but why do you look so sad?"

At that, Anke started to cry softly. The matron entered—she must have been eavesdropping—and announced the interview was at an end. She whisked the girl away. "Perhaps at a later date you will be able to talk to her again."

They saw three more girls that afternoon. One talked only about hiking and the salt air. Another, named Lotte, mentioned what she called the "night life". Parties around a campfire weren't uncommon, she said, and then, with a smile growing almost seductively beneath her blue eyes and blonde hair, she said one of the most handsome camp instructors was clearly falling in love with her.

"Don't look shocked," she said after Humph raised his eyebrow. "I'm nineteen. I'm old enough for anything. Yes?"

The look on Duffy's face differed from that on Humph's. He was clearly appraising Lotte.

"Reprobate," thought Humph.

Together, he and Duffy asked her about the classroom aspect of their days on Long Island.

"It's just like regular school in New York," said Lotte. "But we talk mostly about Germany. History, current events. Those of us who need it also get advanced German lessons."

"Sounds very interesting," said Duffy, more sardonically than sincerely. Lotte didn't pick up on it. She was apparently in full "good girl" mode.

"And if we are caught not paying attention or not completing our assignments, we get the ruler."

"You get beaten?" Humph asked.

"Yes," said Lotte. "And very hard, too."

The third girl presented by the matron was tall and skinny. Her name was Britta. Duffy later told Humph that Britta was definitely the party-pooper type.

As if she'd been prepared, Britta recited the Bund's primary activities, the rallies staged across the country. She stood almost at full attention when stating what the Bund was. She was not at all nervous, just sincere.

"The Bund's purpose is to promote our ideology, that is, Nazi ideology in this country. One of the methods is anti-Semitism. We organize rallies and events that emulate Nazi ceremonies. They also teach us about communications. The Bund's activities include parades in full Nazi regalia, propaganda effort and, of course, camps like this one. We have tens of thousands of members."

While delivering her little speech, she looked straight into Humph's eyes, which pleased Humph because it likely meant she accepted him as a fellow German, based on what the matron had told her.

As the interview came to an end, she retained complete composure when asked if corporal punishment was used in the school.

13

"Of course it is, sir. There are many frivolous young people here. Such people cannot serve our purpose. Americans are a lax people. Some of them are also very promiscuous by Nazi standards."

"Of course. Of course," said Humph.

Britta's acceptance of him emboldened him.

"What useful things do you learn here, Britta?"

She answered that they learned military things, like sending encoded signals, deciphering signals, gaining entry into factories and offices.

"Do all your fellow students appreciate the value of these teachings as you do?"

"Not all," she answered. "Even though some German-American parents are among us, I suspect not all of them knew at the outset, when they joined the Bund, how militaristic we are. Consequently, we think their children come to camp thinking it will be like the Boy Scouts or Girl Guides. The reality of the world is impressed upon them from their arrival."

"Dankeschön." Humph thanked her profusely for all her useful information about the camp.

"One last question," he asked. "With so many thousands of young people here at any given time, it would seem to me natural for there to be the occasional occurrence of passion gone too far, if I may put it that way. Earlier today, we met a seriously depressed young woman with a severe bruise on her face, as if she'd been punched, and eyes that all but refused to look into ours. Do you know anything about this poor woman? You are clearly a highly principled woman. A truthful answer will serve our purpose to no end."

"Goddamn brilliant," thought Duffy. "He's made an ally of dear, severe Britta."

"Yes, sir," Britta answered. "She was raped by an older man. That's all I know."

Britta then turned smartly on her heel and left the room.

Before heading back to Manhattan, Humph and Duffy wandered around the grounds. On the surface, it looked like any other summer camp, young people in bathing attire running to the water, a teenage boy doing acrobatic summersaults, a man who appeared to be a supervisor. Despite the heat, he wore an Italian Fascist-style blackshirt. Earlier, when they had arrived at the camp, Duffy pointed out two men in official brownshirts. He said he'd seen shirts like that in a cinema newsreel. "I think the narrator called them storm troopers or something like that."

The most chilling evidence of Nazi ideology were the shrubs trimmed to form swastikas.

When Duffy noticed them, he said: "Humph, kindly make sure we get back to America before the sun sets tonight." It was a hot morning, but the sight was chilling.

Before leaving, Humph went back to the camp office to ask if camp members stayed there the whole summer.

"No, few do. Many come and go all summer long, though. There's nothing to stop them from leaving unless they're following some kind of training course." Humph again affected a slight German accent and asked what courses were available. He was handed a pamphlet. The first ones listed were predictable ones like sailing, swimming and organized hikes. When he turned the page, he found exactly what Britta had mentioned, things like wireless communication, the use of codes and other wartime skills.

Humph held up the pamphlet and pointed toward the courses on page 2.

"Those," said the man behind the counter, "are compulsory. They are required for membership in the Bund, which sponsors the camp. Once enrolled, you have to complete them before returning to New York."

While Humph read through the rest of the pamphlet, Duffy stepped up to the counter and asked if there was anywhere where a thirsty man could sample "your world-renowned German beers."

"Absolutely, mein Herr." The subject was clearly close to the heart of the man behind the counter. "Just walk back to town and follow the signs to Goebbels Strasse."

Once outside, Humph couldn't hold back a grin. Duffy always found a way to sniff out beer.

"Research, Humph, research," Duffy hurried to say.

Faced with a wait for the LIRR train back to town, the two men sampled several beers. After each, Duffy pronounced judgment. Each passed his strict standards.

Humph had remained mostly silent while Duffy pursued his research. Finally, he broke the silence and said they would have to return tomorrow. "That girl, the one with the bruises, something tells me we need to talk to her again. In fact, I'd dearly love to find a way to get her back to the city where she could talk freely."

"What are you thinking?" asked Duffy.

"The teaching of Nazi ideology isn't the only dark thing going on here. I can't put my finger on it, but my gut says I shouldn't give up."

CHAPTER 3

HUMPH went to sleep looking for a way to convince the Bund camp to allow him to bring the woman, named Anke, to Manhattan. He had explained her situation, the evident beating, to Rebecca.

His wife had joined Humph in several pre-supper drinks. The Scotches had no effect on Humph, but as fit as she was, Rebecca was tipsy. But as Humph knew from decades of investigational experience, booze can liberate the mind on occasion.

"What," began Rebecca, planting her index finger on Humph's chest, "if we hired a motorboat and put-putted close to the shore where," she said, stabbing Humph's chest again, "we had pre-arranged for Anke to do her daily German physical education exercises? She would probably be with other girls doing the same, and no one would be watching her in particular.

"You or Duff would be lurking nearby. In my mind, Humph, both you and Duff are wearing bathing costumes. At the opportune moment, you guys grab her and carry her to the motorboat. From there, we slice through Long Island Sound waters at record-breaking speed until we are beyond the Hamptons and entering truly American territory. You all would then board the next train to Manhattan, making sure it wasn't a homeward-bound Camp Siegfried special."

Rebecca, now sitting on Humph's chest, continued: "I am assuming that Anke will be happy to be off the island, and she won't start screaming that she's been kidnapped. We could put her up, Humph, or maybe Eve would be happy to help a fellow rape victim."

Many years before, Eve, a stripper and a burlesque performer as her mother had been, was kidnapped and raped by a gang of bootleggers that operated brothels throughout the city.

Humph pulled Rebecca's face toward his and kissed her long and hard. She'd outdone herself. Her mind had instantly gone where Humph's hadn't.

"My beautiful partner, thanks to you, we now have a plan."

He slept like a baby.

Humph and Duff returned to Penn Station early the following morning only to find that the Camp Siegfried special ran only on weekends. However, a ticket agent explained it was still a regular LIRR stop. The nice thing, they discovered on boarding, was that the train wasn't crowded, and German accents no longer dominated and no one sang songs from the Fatherland.

Once at the camp, Humph walked into the camp office and asked casually whether Lotte was around. The man behind the counter looked at a clipboard and announced that she was at the archery field.

"Bitte," said Humph.

They had no trouble finding her. She and five other students were demonstrating extraordinary accuracy. They waited for an instructor-ordered pause and approached the young woman.

Lotte expressed no surprise at seeing the two men from New York. She was as matter-of-fact as during the first meeting. No "hello", no "have a good day".

"Anke? Yes, I saw her a while ago. She's on the beach somewhere. Look for a bunch of kayaks on the beach." With that she pulled another arrow from her quiver.

A few minutes later, Humph spotted the kayaks. Duffy was finding walking over sand to be a challenge for his lungs. Humph slowed down.

Once there, they watched the class. The instructor finished his spiel, and one by one, a Hitler-youth-in-the-making hauled a kayak into the water. They idled their way closer to the launch spot. Duffy was the first to spot Anke. He first looked back and saw the instructor packing his gear.

"Now, Humph!"

They rushed to Anke. Humph grabbed her shoulders and thrust his face in front of hers so she hopefully would recognize him as not being an enemy. Before any of the other students could respond, he and Duffy were several steps into the water. The motorboat drifted right up to them. Duffy got in, held out his arms for the girl, then Humph, hoping not to capsize the motorboat with his bulk, succeeded in climbing on board. The motorboat's engine roared to life.

From that point, everything went according to plan. The wait for a train was thirty minutes. It seemed like an eternity, but sitting shoulder to shoulder with the two older men seemed to make Anke feel safe.

Almost two hours later, they got out of a taxi at Tompkins Square. Rebecca must have been looking out the window because the door was already open behind her as Anke and the two PIs exited the cab. As they mounted the steps, Rebecca announced that Eve was already there. "She's all in for caring for Anke."

Even after Eve and Rebecca escorted Anke to the comfortable sofa, it was clear the young woman was traumatized. Eve sat next to her and held her hand. Rebecca asked if she would like tea or coffee or something stronger. Anke answered:

"Schnapps?" She said it as if no one would understand her request. Humph, because of his upbringing, came to the rescue.

"We only have European schnapps. Would that be OK?"

For the first time, Anke smiled.

"That would be perfect."

Duffy looked perplexed.

"Schnapps is schnapps, no?"

No, said Humph, handing Duffy a Scotch. "American schnapps is not as strong, and it's sweetened. I think, after what she's gone through, Anke needs something to bring her back to earth."

Anke was smiling at what Humph said.

Humph didn't press her with tough questions. Instead, Eve and Rebecca plied her with stories about working on Broadway, which Anke seemed to marvel at. Humph decided to wait until the next day before interrogating her about the rape and the murdered man of German descent in Manhattan.

After she left with Eve, Humph phoned Detective Higgins to set up an hour to meet in the next couple of days. He was out of the office.

He and Rebecca called it a day and walked to their favorite diner for some bare-bones American food. Rebecca knew Humph's ways of unwinding and didn't object.

When Humph arrived at Eve's place to talk to the victim-suspect, he found Anke relaxed. They sat across from each other at the kitchen table. Eve handed her "dad" a coffee. "Apparently," she said with a laugh, "it's not up to German standards."

Anke quickly said she meant no insult. "The coffee is fine, just different from what I've grown up with."

"May I be blunt, Anke? We have two cases to settle, and bluntness is the fastest way to do so."

"Please," she said.

"My first concern," said Humph, "is this: Were you raped at camp?"

"Yes."

"Who raped you?"

There was a long pause.

Humph broke the silence:

"Was it Otto Schmidt?"

Anke gasped.

"Yes."

"What was he to you?"

"He was my guidance counselor, or at least that's what they called people like him."

"What were guidance counselors supposed to do?"

"Teach us German skills."

"What are German skills? You're American."

"You don't understand. We had to learn skills to help Germany win any battle that might come in the future. That included speaking German like a German. I was beaten several times for my use of American expressions. I was also beaten for refusing to learn how to fire a gun."

"Anything else?"

Anke took a long time to answer. Humph didn't press.

"Yes, sir. I was beaten for refusing to bed a certain man. A Mr. Schmidt. He called his superior. I was bound to a bed. The two of them stood over me like ancient devils."

"What do you mean?"

"Like devils in Der Freischütz. It's an opera about gruesome supernatural things. It's horrible."

"What did they do to you?"

"At the time, nothing, but they said one of the main purposes of the summer camp was to create Aryan babies, American children born of pure German parents. A week later, Schmidt raped me. I fought back, but he beat me with his big fist. He is more than twice my size. There was no one to complain to at the camp, no police. I was told coupling was part of my duties for the Bund."

"Would you like to take a pause, Anke?"

"No. I want this to be over with."

Almost reluctantly, Humph brought up Schmidt's murdered body.

"Were you at the scene?" he asked.

"Yes. I was the one who killed him." The stark admission froze Humph and Duffy. Neither said a word. They just stared at the girl. "Someone at the camp told me he was going to kill me. Other girls have been killed. I ran away, back to Manhattan. I didn't dare go home. My family lives in Yorkdale. I was living on the street on the Lower East Side. Somehow, after several days, he found me.

"I shot him from a yard away. I was hiding behind boxes near a loading dock on the East River. I fled the camp in a boat. That's where they took me. A young sailor said he would be in town for two weeks. He was Austrian and spoke German. He asked if I needed a weapon. He leant me his gun. He was a sweet boy."

"Why would he help you like that?"

Anke paused before answering.

"Are you Americans that ignorant? I'm sorry, but Hitler, a madman to be sure, was also Austrian. His fucking country annexed Austria three years ago. Just like that. The boy who gave me the gun was just defending his country. The world would forgive him."

Humph closed his notebook. In his mind, he cursed America for not having entered the war. But that wasn't why he was here, interrogating a young woman with German blood on her hands.

"I understand. It was self-defense, sort of."

"Sort of?" she asked.

"In the sense that he didn't have a gun pointed at you. You just shot him on sight."

Anke went silent.

"We'll go to the police together. I'll explain all the circumstances to them. Trust me."

Her shoulders sagged. Humph took her hand and led her to Eve's room.

"Eve will take good care of you. You can trust her. She's been where you are now."

"Eve knows all the horrors."

"I must ask, why are you so willing to plead guilty to murder?"

"I was raised to be honest in all things. My American mother taught me that. My German father would only say that the world was complicated. It was like he was caught between two worlds and couldn't decide. He was not a bad man. At least, that's what my mom said."

CHAPTER 4

THE head precinct detective, Higgins, welcomed his friend the next morning.

"It's been ages."

"No work," said Humph. "No cases. No fun."

"Sorry to hear that," the detective answered. Then, with a rare Scottish smile, he added:

"How can you be bored with a wife like Rebecca?"

Humph couldn't help laughing.

"Thank you for the reminder. I'm indeed the luckiest flatfoot in the world."

"Henry," he continued, "I come to you with extraordinary information about a case already on your books. Do you remember that German guy you found not so long ago, a guy named Schmidt?"

Higgins had to think for a minute.

"Yeah, vaguely. Because we had no other answer, we suspected it was a gang killing."

Humph had been under the same impression when he and Duffy went to the crime scene.

"Look, Henry, I've come into possession of information that suggests an alternate version of the crime. I'd like to go into more detail but I'm a bit perplexed by it at the moment. Would you agree to a pub consultation tomorrow or the day after?"

Higgins stared hard at Humph, but Humph's face never twitched.

"You wouldn't be withholding evidence, would you?"

"To be honest, I don't know."

"OK, Humph. See you tomorrow at 2 p.m. around the corner."

"Around the corner" meant the cop tavern less than two blocks away.

That night, after Humph and Rebecca had gone to bed, Humph released a big sigh and said he needed her opinion.

He recited the facts:

"The girl is guilty of murder but . . .

"She had reason to fear for her life . . .

"She had already been raped by the dead man . . .

"She confessed freely and made no effort to deny the facts . . .

"And most important of all, I think she can provide valuable evidence of other crimes being committed at the camp by German fanatics."

Rebecca stared at Humph in disbelief. "You needed me to verify your case to not prosecute her? What's wrong with you?"

"I like my reputation as a hardline kind of guy who puts the law before everything."

Rebecca laughed.

"If I believed you felt that way, I would never have married you. Life does not shape itself to fit the law.

26

Extenuating circumstances are worth their weight in gold. I'll opt for them anytime. Otherwise, all my friends would be in jail."

"Goodnight, judge," said Humph, turning on his side and presenting his back to her.

At the tavern the next afternoon, Humph showed unusual signs of reticence. Higgins wanted no part of it.

"I'm a busy man today, Humph. Out with it."

Humph swallowed and then spewed.

"I have in my custody a young woman who readily admits to having murdered Mr. Schmidt near the East River docks two months ago. She even possesses the gun that she fired. Ordinarily, Henry, I would have handed her straight over to your boys for incarceration and trial. However . . ."

Humph paused. He then raised one finger to the barkeep. "Triple Scotch, and take away the beer before me." Then an afterthought: "Unless you want it, Henry."

The detective did not hesitate:

"I somehow feel I will need it."

"The woman, the girl, she's eighteen, almost nineteen," said Humph, "she's German-American."

"So are you, if I'm not mistaken."

"The difference," said Humph, "is that the German part of me has virtually nothing to do with who I am. For this young lady, or at least for her parents, it is everything.

"She lives with them on the Upper East Side, on York Avenue, around 87ᵗʰ Street, if memory serves. A lot of German-Americans live up there, the ones who have been able to turn their backs on the poverty of the Lower East Side and become middle class."

Higgins was truly grumpy.

"Why do I care right now where she lives?"

"Was your porridge too salty this morning? Just listen, please. I'll get to the point."

Humph told him about his discovery of some monstrous

organization, called the German-American Bund.

Higgins said he knew about them already.

"They held a massive gathering recently at Madison Square Garden. Tens of thousands of Nazi lovers and haters of Jews and socialists. But, Humph, to my knowledge, they haven't broken any laws. Free speech and all that."

Humph admitted that Higgins had beaten him to the punch. He said he'd never heard of the Bund until he started nosing around after hearing about Camp Siegfried on Long Island from his buddy at the New York World-Telegram.

"For God's sake, Henry, they even have a street named Hitler," Humph added.

"Didn't know that," said the detective. "Go on, Humph."

Humph explained that the discovery left him both outraged and curious. He described the visit he made to the camp with Duffy. It was Duffy's idea, he said, that he recall his own distant German heritage and polish up what little German he knew. As well as Nazi street names, he said, there were hedges trimmed to look like swastikas.

"Faking a German accent wasn't too hard. For once, Duff kept his mouth shut, and I did all the talking when we made enquiries at the camp office. We pretended to be interested in all their summer camp activities for young people. Then I said I'd like to meet some of them. The camp employee, coordinator, whatever, was quite accommodating. She collared four young women, probably not yet even twenty, and one at a time asked them to answer any questions I might have about the camp. One of them, a girl named Anke, was extremely withdrawn. Her face was badly bruised. We didn't get anything out of her until talking with the final girl, totally unemotional, matter-of-fact, almost soldierly. She told us that the bruised girl had been beaten by an instructor and that such beatings were relatively commonplace."

Humph added that the fourth girl suggested such consequences were necessary in order to ensure discipline.

She didn't explain why there had to be discipline at a summer camp for adolescents.

"Duffy and I found a saloon offering fine German beer. The camp official recommended it to us. We sat there for some time comparing impressions of the camp."

"And drinking," Higgins interjected.

"Of course," said Humph with a smile.

"Long story short, Henry, I couldn't turn my back on that girl who'd been so badly beaten. The next day, Duff and I returned to the camp and asked to see her again."

Higgins took a sip of his drink, raising his index finger at the same time.

"Now is when you repeat the phrase 'long story short' before continuing."

Humph obliged:

"The girl freely admitted to Rebecca and me that she murdered Schmidt. She still has the gun she used. It had belonged to Schmidt."

Instantly, he had Higgins's attention.

"Where is this girl now?"

"At our place," said Humph. "Or, by now, perhaps at Eve's. I thought Eve was the best person to console Anke."

"For heaven's sake, Humph, why didn't you bring this Anke girl straight to me? She's a confessed murderer."

Humph paused.

Finally, he said:

"How do you spell 'extenuating circumstances'?"

Higgins remained silent.

"First, she's a rape victim. The dead man did that, and he beat the crap out of her to boot.

"Second, the guy was drunk when he stopped under the bridge. The girl knew the odds were good that he'd rape her again.

"Third, she saw this bastard's gun under his jacket. He was so drunk his words were barely intelligible. He was cursing her for no immediate reason. There was no expectation that he would ignore her until he sobered up enough to drive more than fifty miles back to the camp, or figure out how to get to a ferry to return.

"She grabbed his gun and got out of the car. A minute later, this Schmidt guy had staggered while getting out of the car. He turned to face Anke and started plodding toward her. Bang!" said Humph. "What do you call that, Henry? If you say murder, I'm going to walk out of here and make sure you guys never find her."

Higgins had listened closely.

"Not a chance, my friend. You're right. This is not a murder. But I still have to talk to her, and I need the gun. We'll decide what to do afterward."

An hour later, the patrol car pulled up at Eve's place.

Anke ran toward the back door leading to the fire escape. Eve all but tackled her. Lying on the floor, Eve pressed Anke's face to hers.

"Sweetie, we're all going to make things turn out all right. Trust me, dear."

Anke was trembling when Eve led her into the living room to meet the police and Humph.

"Anke," said Humph gently, "I've had a long talk with the chief of detectives. He knows you had reason to shoot Schmidt. You're not being charged with murder. But we have to follow procedures for now. We're not going to abandon you."

The cops handcuffed her. Humph reassured her that he had been a cop for many years. The cuffs didn't mean anything for the moment.

"It's just procedure. We can't fight everything all at once. Come along, dear."

Humph remained at her side as she was led to the patrol car.

"I'll see you downtown," he said after she'd sat down in the back seat.

CHAPTER 5

HUMPH was kicking himself for not knowing about Camp Siegfried. Higgins called him in and told him what their files contained. Simply put, the camp was training operatives, young German-Americans trained in espionage techniques. The fun-and-sun activities were just a cover. The camp, which attracted thousands of visitors each summer, was a school for spies.

"The State Department is looking into this matter," Humph told him, meaning it was not beyond the scope of NYPD investigations.

Two months later, in September, Anke was found not guilty in the killing of Schmidt. The court ruled there were insufficient grounds to pursue the charge of murder.

After the trial, Anke asked Eve if she could stay with her a little longer. Her parents, she said, were rabid Nazis.

Eve said yes.

The two had bonded. No one knew better than Eve how the world could turn your life upside down and make you someone unrecognizable to everyone who knew you, even family. She'd been kidnapped, turned into a prostitute and an accomplice for gangsters. Her success on Broadway later on was a simple testament to willpower and an ability to have faith in dreams.

Anke, in Eve's mind, was a passionate young woman who never for a moment thought of how evil people can be. She had led an obscenely sheltered life. Eve had no real experience with parents, but her own powerful sense of independence told her that parents were oppressively ignorant about the world their children were entering— even at Camp Siegfried.

After all, it was Anke's parents who had sent her there. She had been such a dutiful daughter that she'd never suspected for a minute that her parents would subject her to brainwashing in order to satisfy their own political beliefs. She had gone to the camp to learn archery, nothing more. It was, after all, a noble, ancient, Olympic sport. She could make her parents proud.

In just months, all those dutiful dreams had turned to a heap of hypocrisy.

To help Anke re-enter the world, Eve frequently took her to watch her rehearsals and performances on the world's greatest stage. Anke was dumbfounded by this new world that was both glittery and gritty. The competition among performers was ferocious at first, at least until roles had been awarded. Then the rehearsals proved to be unforgiving tests of endurance. Anke was in awe of the world Eve called home.

Humph visited Eve several times that month. Anke was starting to become a new person. There was some confidence. She could also look into your eyes as you spoke. That was a huge progression from the day he had met her on Long Island.

Humph also rejoiced in seeing Eve and Anke embrace and dance together like teenage girls often do.

In October, all that changed. Federal agents knocked on the door. A steel curtain had descended. Their lives were imprisoned.

Eventually, Humph and Eve were released from the suffocating dome. Anke wasn't.

When Humph felt part of his normal world, he begged to see Detective Higgins instantly.

"Tell me this isn't happening," he said. His voice was close to a scream.

"Humph, my friend, this has nothing to do with me or NYPD. It's a federal charge."

"What charge? How is this possible? My daughter and Anke have been together every day since her acquittal."

Higgins took an eternity before voicing a reply.

"Espionage, Humph. Anke has been charged with espionage."

"How the hell is that possible?" shouted Humph. "Eve and I have been with her all the time."

Higgins explained.

"She's been under surveillance by the FBI from even before the murder. She and a bunch of other kids."

Humph deflated. He opened his mouth, and no sound ensued.

This was impossible, he thought. His instincts were never wrong. This girl was innocent. She was a child in a world that didn't acknowledge innocence.

Higgins said nothing.

Finally, Humph said that the girl hadn't returned to the camp since moving to Eve's place.

"The feds, Humph, they're saying that she spied with the other kids before you even met her."

"No, no, no!"

"It's out of my hands," said Higgins.

Humph raised himself from the chair in front of the detective's desk. Like a robot, he moved toward the stairs. Higgins felt paralyzed to see his friend and an investigator he thought of as highly as anyone who'd ever worn the NYPD uniform.

He descended the stairs after Humph.

The huge man had disappeared.

CHAPTER 6

ON his way home, Humph picked up the day's papers. The Nazis had bombed Belfast, their second attack on Ireland. He also saw that America's first peacetime draft, initiated the previous year under the Selective Training and Service Act, was bearing fruit. Was the American tide turning in favor of joining the war? He still had his doubts. At least the government, already sending armaments and supplies to Europe in greater and greater quantities, wasn't twiddling its thumbs in the face of what might turn out to be the worst conflagration in history. People used to say the First World War was the war to end all wars. Clearly they were wrong. The Nazis were already proving that mankind's evil knows no limits.

On the way home, he dropped by Duffy's unannounced. Duffy hated that. He insisted on the right to manage his coherent hours.

It turned out that he was home and sober.

Before Humph could utter a word, Duffy exclaimed: "Belfast! Fucking Belfast!"

At the outset of Nazi expansion in Europe, Duffy joined most Americans in believing that "those silly European buggers" could do what they wanted. "They all deserve whatever happens to them," he once said. "They keep declaring war on each other because some hoity-toity asshole perceived an insult somewhere along the line. Been doing that for centuries, the whole lot of them."

Humph didn't say anything, but he was relieved that Duffy was coming around to his view that America had to act. It didn't really matter that it took Nazi attacks on his homeland to turn the tide.

Humph wanted a drink. After his interview with the lawyer, he had a lot to think about and plan in order to save Anke. However, he hesitated to ask for one. In some ways, a sober Duffy was a blessing. In the end, though, he decided that an imbibing Irishman was the real man.

Duffy served him and himself. Duffy nestled into the corner of his old sofa as if he sensed that Humph had an endless sermon to deliver.

Humph recounted everything Anke's lawyer had to say hours earlier. The detail made Duffy wonder whether Humph was planning on going before the Supreme Court himself to defend the pretty German-American girl. Finally, Humph wound down his rhetoric and said their job—"You and me, Duff"—was to first of all investigate the hell out of the girl's life. "We have to be able to show that she has been deprived of freedom of thought and action for years. I want to show that she was a mere puppet, a dutiful daughter seeking parental approval."

Duffy paused with an index finger in the air. "May I speak, lawyer Humph?"

Humph laughed. Never in his life had Duffy asked for permission before expressing his opinion.

Duffy said he had no trouble accepting that the pert blonde felt obliged to do her parents' will, but what about the espionage, he asked.

The next day, Humph went to the FBI's New York headquarters on Church Street and Barclay. For the long-legged Humph, it was a relatively short walk. He was too angry to negotiate by phone.

Once he'd established his former NYPD credentials, Humph was shown into an interview room. He'd hoped to be taken to an office, an office occupied by a supervising agent with some authority to act.

Instead, he had to spend time detailing the case to a young agent who had not even started to shave.

"Well, sir, let me look into this. I could have a coffee brought to you while you wait."

"I'd accept a whiskey, but I suspect the FBI doesn't have any."

The agent, backing out of the room like a bureaucratic slave, left the room.

Thirty-seven minutes later, according to Humph's timepiece, a secretary led him to an office. The agent said he was familiar with the case.

Humph politely introduced himself. Then after taking the chair the agent pointed to, he took aim and fired:

"You have charged a woman with espionage and taken her into custody. I have gotten to know this woman through my own investigation. Anything she may have done was clearly under duress. She's a teenager. She was abused, beaten and raped. And she was forced by the man who raped her to commit an act of espionage. New York courts have already found her not guilty of murdering this man by reason of self-defense. Now you ignore all this evidence of coercion and charge her with espionage. No American girl facing such abuse could have refused to do their captor's bidding. She deserves compassion. The courts have already shown that. It is now your turn to acknowledge that."

The agent didn't respond.

Humph, slightly calmer after having stated the facts, added:

"Like every freedom-loving American, I applaud the FBI's efforts to eliminate espionage taking place in our country. But to try to polish your image among the American people by prosecuting every Tom, Dick and Harry you encounter won't stand the test of justice. Back off and examine the facts, the human facts, for God's sake."

The agent said:

"I can assure you, sir, that our investigations are based on fact."

Humph was ready to explode, but he knew that would hurt his cause.

"I am an investigator, too, and I know this case better than you or any of your boys. There is no case to be made against her. She's a child, for God's sake, who was viciously compromised by adult Nazi sympathizers. She deserves our sympathy, not our condemnation."

The agent didn't have a reply.

Humph rose from his chair.

"Where is she being held?"

"At the Tombs."

The Tombs was the infamous New York detention center for people awaiting trial. They could be left there for ages.

In a calm voice, Humph said:

"Thank you, agent. I'll meet her there. If your people pursue this case further, be forewarned that it will not end well for the FBI. As I'm sure you know, there have already been stories in the press about how your well-intentioned efforts to round up spies has turned out to be amateurish and ineffective."

The agent remained silent. Humph walked out.

When he got home an hour later, he received a phone call. Higgins.

"I hear you called the FBI a bunch of embarrassing amateurs, bunglers . . . all that sort of thing. And that you essentially threatened them if they pursued this case."

"Essentially, Higgins, your summation is accurate. And please know that I have no intention of apologizing."

Higgins knew this wasn't the moment to negotiate with Humph.

"Wouldn't think of asking you to apologize. It's just that the agent you berated was under the impression that you represented the NYPD."

Humph laughed at the politics of inter-agency relations.

"I did not represent myself as NYPD. The guy just assumed it. It didn't serve my purpose to correct him, idiot that he seemed to be."

Clearly, Humph was still steaming. He was usually polite to a fault, a characteristic that made him unusually successful during interrogations when he was still an NYPD officer. Higgins himself had commended the practice as revolutionary compared to the conventional wisdom of threatening and beating suspects until they said what you wanted to hear.

Higgins suspected the conversation would be short. To his surprise, a becalmed Humph posed a question:

"It's a clear-cut case of coercions and a threat of physical violence, if not death itself, against a teenager, a girl who had no means of escaping any of the consequences threatened. It seems from my research, my friend, that extenuating circumstances means shit in the eyes of federal court judges. How is that possible?"

"I can't answer that," said Higgins. "But that's the way things are."

"Then find me a goddamned lawyer who understands this kind of injustice," Humph said, almost yelling.

Two days later, Higgins sent a telegram to Humph.

"Found a lawyer who might be sympathetic. He's an American, but he has lived in Europe and speaks passable

German. His name is Begovich, or at least that's how it's pronounced. First name is Novak."

It took a week before Humph got a date to meet the lawyer.

To his surprise, Begovich was fully informed about the girl's case. It turned out that Higgins had talked to him and in passing explained that a certain detective's family was outraged by the court's decision and was preparing to continue caring for the girl if in prison.

Humph nodded appreciatively. He owed Higgins no matter where the case went.

"Where do we go from here?" asked Humph.

"She will stay in the Tombs, but I'm going to do my utmost to keep her there so you can maintain contact. Higgins told me about your family taking her in. I'm going to find every bit of case law that recognizes coercion in the commission of a federal crime. But it will take time. I have a small practice. I don't have access to a team of clerks to investigate."

Humph nodded, although he had been hoping for a more hopeful answer.

"But, sir, you have every right to visit her in the Tombs. Tell her you have me on your side. I have a reputation for being tenacious. A lot of people don't like me, but I get results."

Humph decided he trusted the man.

The Tombs had a reputation as one of the worst detention centers in America. It was connected to the old Manhattan Criminal Courts Building with a passageway known as the "Bridge of Sighs" that crossed four stories above Franklin Street.

The lawyer told Humph he was able to get Anke held there instead of in a potentially distant federal lock-up by filing a notice of appeal indicating he intended to challenge the conviction.

"I took it upon myself to pay the filing fee and order

transcripts of the trial proceedings to prepare my appeal. That all comes out of my pocket, by the way, the fee and the transcripts."

"We'll make good on all your expenses. We've got two families who want justice for Anke."

The lawyer nodded his thanks, then began explaining what he'd have to come up with to make the appeals court consider the case. It was a complicated laundry list. He first said he'd have to find legal errors.

"So far, I've seen none, but I've got a lot more reading and rereading to do. However, I already feel strongly, Humph, that your Madchen Anke did not receive effective assistance of counsel. It was as if her lawyer simply wanted to lump her in with the sixteen or seventeen other people being charged with espionage in the same case. He never raised the extenuating circumstances we talked about, you know, the rape and the beatings. I want you to know, Humph, that in my mind she is a victim pure and simple. Her rights have been violated."

He paused for a glass of water.

"Finally, Humph, what has shocked me most as a lawyer is that Anke's counsel never called the several witnesses who had declared they were willing to testify that the dead man, the instructor, had raped and beaten her on multiple occasions. Why on earth they didn't, I'll never know. Under these circumstances, there is no way Anke could be said to have carried out an act of espionage willingly."

Humph was impressed. The lawyer told him it would take possibly months to settle the case, and there was even the possibility that the federal court ruling would be set aside.

"What we need in the meantime," said Begovich, "is additional evidence of coercion. I mean by that, every scrap of evidence, circumstantial or empirical. We need to investigate her teenage schoolmates, boyfriends and, most of all, her parents. How pro-Nazi are they? When did they start indoctrinating her?"

"Understood," said Humph.

The next day, Humph wasn't sure why, but he wanted to visit the company that was the victim of espionage, the Sperry Corporation, by Anke and the others.

According to an account he'd read in the *Daily News*, Anke had tried to obtain a job at the Sperry Gyroscope Corporation on Flatbush Avenue in Brooklyn. The company manufactured various military and naval equipment such as bomb sights.

However, evidence presented in court showed that while she applied for a job at Sperry, she never got it.

It was, to Bergovitch's mind, at that point that conjecture became absurd. He had explained to Humph, via the *Daily News* clipping because he didn't yet have the transcripts in hand, that Anke was arrested one night in Manhattan. Apparently, she had an espionage boss named Ludwig or something like that, the lawyer said. The FBI eagerly pounced on Anke, claiming she had been used as a sexual lure for American servicemen.

"How did she contact them?" he asked Humph. "I'll tell you how the FBI says she did. This boss, Ludwig, would go out for drives and find American servicemen hitchhiking. He would offer rides that they'd eagerly accept. People hitchhiked all the time. But lo and behold, in the car with Ludwig was this attractive eighteen-year-old who, according to the FBI, had no other purpose than seducing them for military information."

Almost as an aside, the lawyer mentioned Ludwig's past.

"Some years ago, he worked for the Nazi Party in Germany or Austria. I can't remember which at the top of my head. Regardless, he was no amateur spy."

The lawyer's version made him believe all the more in the girl's innocence. The FBI, in search of positive publicity in its fight to protect Americans from the Nazis, had created a story even Hollywood would reject.

Duffy said he wasn't up to accompanying Humph to Sperry's Brooklyn headquarters. Anyway, Humph said, he was just going to cross the t's and dot the i's.

The building was imposing. It was not a skyscraper, just a wide, multistoried building that represented solidarity and trust to investors.

Humph had to pass through a legion of executives before reaching someone who could talk about the espionage case in federal court. His name was Dalton Whynot.

They sat down and a secretary served very fresh coffee, as if she'd made it when Humph walked onto the floor.

Humph congratulated him on the coffee. The executive beamed. "We're doing very well these days, sir. Though we're not yet at war, our sales are skyrocketing, if I can say that. Government contracts, of course."

Humph explained that he was investigating the recent case of espionage.

"I know exactly the case you mean. The FBI really came to the rescue. Everyone convicted, if I remember correctly."

"To be frank, sir," said Humph, "we believe at least one of those convicted of espionage is innocent. Maybe more."

"Detective, hold on a minute. In my book, if the FBI says guilty, they're guilty. Hoover himself swore to the American people he'd rout out America's enemies. We could all sleep well."

"Sir, I'm sure thanks to the FBI we can all sleep well, but the wrongful conviction of individuals, American citizens, no less, doesn't make me sleep well. We have rights. That's why we love America, right, sir? We have rights other countries never dreamed of."

Dalton Whynot let go of his suspenders and leaned forward over his desk.

"Well, sir, you put your point well, patriotically well."

Humph went on to explain that the felon who concerned him was an eighteen-year-old girl who applied for a job at his company but was rejected.

Whynot leaned further to reach his intercom.

"Susan!"

Instead of answering the blunt command by intercom, Susan, a middle-aged woman with fidgety hands, entered the office.

"Sir?"

"Do you recall a teenaged girl applying for work here in the past few months?"

After no small amount of stuttering, Susan said she'd have to check on that. She then abruptly left the office.

Whynot affected joviality and said, "We are a big corporation, sir. We hire and fire by the truckload, as you can surely imagine."

Humph could not imagine liking anyone less than the man seated across from him.

When the secretary returned, she handed her boss a slim folder.

After skimming it, Whynot said he now did recall the girl.

"Because of the sensitive nature of our work, as I'm sure you understand, we had to reject her application because there was some question about her citizenship in this great land of ours. She was born in Stuttgart, Germany, came to the United States in 1929 and claimed to be naturalized through her father, with whom she lived."

"Surely that wouldn't be hard to verify," Humph said.

"I didn't handle this application myself, but I assure you I can rely on my staff to protect the company in all instances. We do important work."

Humph realized he wouldn't get anywhere with this corporate dummkopf and took his leave. At least he'd learned that Anke hadn't applied for any job involving security. She had come offering her high school skills with adding machines.

As he rode the train back to Manhattan, he kept wondering about the part of the description in the *New York Daily News* that said the well-dressed young lady exhibited total calm while confessing her guilt.

By the time of her appearance in court, her face bore no bruises from the beatings her camp instructor may have given her. Her plea of guilty did not seem out of place because of her composure. Did Anke see prison as a way to escape the Nazis at Camp Siegfried? Or was she guilty?

CHAPTER 7

REBECCA and Eve were at the kitchen table when Humph got home. They looked at him expectantly. Seeing no reaction, Rebecca stood and kissed him full on. While still pressing herself against him, her hands reached behind his neck and started massaging. Finally, Humph, with his hands on his wife's waist, announced that after the day's investigations, he believed more strongly than ever in Anke's innocence.

"But," he added, "it could take us years to prove it."

He described his session with Begovich, the lawyer. He said he believed absolutely that the lawyer believed 100 percent in her innocence, adding that he was already preparing an appeal.

"He is our greatest friend," he told the girls. "But in the meantime, we have no choice but to maintain our relationship with her through bars at the Tombs. As you might know, ladies, that's the infamous detention center for people awaiting court dates or legal decisions about their cases. The wait can be from weeks to years. It's the best we can do."

Eve jumped in.

"It's simple. One of us goes there to see Anke every day. We won't let her despair, no matter how long it takes." Eve wasn't performing at the moment and had the time. Rebecca was still working demanding hours on Broadway.

Eve was elated they were going to fight for Anke through the courts.

"It's showtime. We're going to war!"

Humph didn't dare tell her that, in his opinion, although he believed in Anke's innocence in the espionage case, victory was a longshot. Convictions weren't overturned on sentiment, just cold, hard law.

Over the following couple of weeks, Humph all but settled into what used to be his neighborhood library— not that it would help Anke's case, but he felt vaguely embarrassed at knowing so little of the German American Bund. He'd of course read about the massive gathering of Nazi supports at Madison Square Garden two years before; more than 20,000 Americans attended in support of the Bund's purpose of spreading Nazi ideology on his side of the ocean. The Bund's goal was to create an American counterpart to the German Nazi Party.

When he and Duffy went to Camp Siegfried, they were astonished to learn that the camp wasn't unique. There were twenty such groups across the country. The groups were organized into about seventy regions. The Bund was vastly larger than Humph had realized.

He expressed his amazement on his first meeting with the lawyer. Begovich offered even more discouraging information. These Nazi-loving Americans believed American values made them a natural ally of Germany.

"So many Americans disliked Jews and socialists and Negros long before the Bund formed. A lot of us Yanks believed the Nazi philosophy was right on the money."

"A horrid thought," said Humph. "By your account of these Americans, I'd find myself at the top of their hate list."

Begovich looked at Humph for a long time, then leaned forward and took Humph's right hand in both of his.

"But they won't win. America can't stay stupid forever."

Before leaving, Humph was happy to hear Begovich say that the State Department and the FBI had been quietly investigating Bund members almost since the organization was founded in 1936.

"Then that gathering at Madison Square Garden opened their eyes even wider. I don't know whether the evidence against Anke and the others was valid on the whole, but I can tell you we'll nail them all soon, maybe even late this year."

"Thank you, my friend," said Humph.

In the following days, Humph continued his reading. More and more, though, he was forced to conclude that life in his city had changed since the bold apparition of Nazi-Americans. While Humph kept up with the war news in Europe, it seemed far away. What he found strange now was his reduced interest in crime in New York. Two nights prior, in front of hundreds of people on 15th Street near First Avenue, a hail of bullets snuffed out the life of Sidney "Shimmy" Sallis. The feds had been hot on his tail after he was indicted along with none other than Bugsy Siegel. Sallis was a member of the Louis (Lepke) Buchalter gang, which the feds wanted to eradicate. However, the mob got to Sallis before the feds could wrap him up in a bow as a star witness.

Normally, Humph would have summed up the development as, "One less bastard to put behind bars." However, with war looming for America, and the appalling number of Americans flashing Nazi colors of late, Humph realized the gangland assassination was the world he knew and was comfortable with. When he talked about his reaction to Rebecca, he finally said he viewed the sidewalk gang wipeout as nostalgic in a way.

After a couple of drinks and some cuddling on the sofa, Rebecca took his chin in her right hand and said, "Humph, no need to feel guilty about your nostalgia. None. I think what is happening with you is simple. You wish our country wasn't on the verge of going to a hideous war. You wish the America you know didn't have Nazi traitors with American citizenship. As messed up as it was, the pre-war America you knew always held out hope of some kind. Now we're entering the dark."

Humph pulled her head to his chest and wrapped his arms around her.

As he released her, he asked:

"Got a job for me on Broadway?"

Rebecca grinned and put her hands on his cheeks.

When she didn't offer him a job, he said:

"Between you and Eve, I've learned that Broadway is forever."

"It is indeed, Humph," said Rebecca. "But remember, it's in your head. That's where Broadway lives. Bombs can't touch it."

What Rebecca said made immense sense, Humph realized. But he knew he could no longer focus on just good old American crime.

The next day he walked to the FBI headquarters on Church Street. The last time he was there, he was trying to get information about the espionage investigation. This time was different.

He introduced himself as usual as a private investigator and former NYPD cop.

"Perhaps I should be talking to someone in your personnel department. I want to work for you to combat espionage in America."

The agent he was talking to was taken aback by the simplicity of the request.

"To my knowledge, sir," the agent replied, "you're at the top of your game, so to speak. I personally have read accounts of several extraordinary cases you've solved. Why on earth do you want to give all that up and work for us?"

Humph took a huge breath and looked at the agent. No words came out. The agent waited.

"I don't wear a flag on my chest," Humph finally said, "but there are threats to our country that leave my blood cold. I'm too damn old to join the armed forces. You're my last hope."

When the agent shuffled papers in a patently meaningly gesture, Humph said:

"Sir, I am an extremely experienced investigator and interrogator. I give you a lieutenant detective on the NYPD as a reference. I have cracked cases his own department couldn't. Why would you possibly hesitate to employ me?"

The agent left the office for a moment. When he returned to his desk, he apologized for not having been able to give Humph an immediate answer.

"The truth is, sir, we're just getting our feet wet in the anti-espionage business. Please don't advertise this fact, but to be honest, we're flying by the seat of our pants at the moment. We don't have authorization from Washington headquarters to hire more agents in this field."

Humph merely nodded at the agent as he walked out the door.

Deflated, Humph decided to resort to his standby cure-all. He spent the rest of the day walking with no destination. More than four hours later, he looked up. The street sign told him where he was. In all that time, he'd paid no attention to where he was. Now he realized some kind of homing pigeon instinct had taken over and pointed him in the direction of the Lower East Side and home.

He then realized he needed to talk to Higgins. When he got home, he phoned the precinct to make an appointment with him.

CHAPTER 8

LIKE everyone from the Lower East Side, Humph knew the name Meyer Lansky. He'd risen to the top of the garbage heap of powerful New York gangsters. Lansky's name had popped into his head while savoring his morning coffee. Rebecca had converted him from Brazilian coffee, America's favorite, to Puerto Rican, which had a more full-bodied flavor than it's South American competitor.

It had been some time since he'd read Lansky's name in the papers. He was sure Higgins would be more up to date. Behind Humph's interest in Lansky was the fact the gangster was Jewish and proud of it. Naturally, figured Humph, he'd hate Nazis.

After seating himself at Higgins's desk, the chief of detectives didn't give him a chance to ask about Lansky. Instead, he wanted to know if Humph could help the NYPD move ahead with several long-standing investigations that had ground to a halt. Humph said he could shed a little bit of light on only one of the cases. The gang member Higgins was after was known to Humph.

"No use looking for him," said Humph. "He was found dead in Jersey a month and a half ago. It wasn't natural causes."

Higgins was happy on the one hand to have a case closed, but he cursed for the millionth time about the total lack of information sharing by neighboring police departments.

"How many, Humph? How many damned hours have my boys wasted looking for a dead man?"

"Same old story, my friend."

Higgins scribbled a note in the file to the effect the case was now closed and tossed it into the out basket on his desk. He then turned to Humph.

"What's on your mind, little guy?" No one but Higgins ever called Humph "little guy".

Humph said he couldn't get his mind off the Long Island Nazi camp and the nationwide Nazi-American rallies.

"They're being held all over the country, for Christ's sake. God knows how many members they have now."

"I know, Humph. We've known about the Bund for a few years."

"Surely we can shut them down."

"As distasteful as they are, they're not breaking any law."

"What about the hate they're spewing? Is that legal? Don't tell me it is."

"Hate to tell you, Humph, but the First Amendment says it is, unless it's directly inciting violence. And that's hard to prove. Our Nazi Yanks have so far mainly contented themselves with sowing the seeds of hatred. That's not an offence."

After getting no response from Humph, Higgins added:

"Our hands are tied."

Humph got up and paced. Higgins was used to it, and his eyes didn't bother to follow the big man's route around his desk.

When Humph landed back in his chair, he asked:

"Meyer Lansky, any sign that he's not OK with this?"

"I invited him for tea and cakes just the other day, but to my great surprise, he didn't show up. You think we're buddies or something, Humph?"

Humph laughed.

"You know what I mean, Higgins. Have Lansky and his boys been spotted at any of the Nazi-American rallies?"

It was almost four o'clock.

"Why don't we adjourn downstairs?"

Downstairs meant the pub precinct down the street.

There was no argument from Humph.

Once settled in with a Scotch for Humph and a hearty ale for the Scottish detective, Higgins said as if there had been no break in their conversation at the precinct:

"In fact, yes. Several times. They've been very active. They tried to disrupt proceedings at the big Madison Square Garden rally that first got your attention. There were more than a few broke Nazi-Yankee noggins that night. Lansky's boys have also been faithful attendees at numerous New Jersey gatherings."

Humph admitted he was glad to hear it.

"You condone vigilante behavior? I'm shocked."

"Evidently, you remember that I was raised by Jews."

Higgins laughed. "Just teasing, my friend."

They ordered another round. Before the waiter arrived, Higgins said:

"What I'm going to say is hush-hush, Humph. The U.S. Department of the Navy has informed us that they are taking these pro-Nazi gatherings very seriously, and they're taking whatever measures they can to disrupt them. The name of a certain Mr. M. Lansky turned up. The explanation from the Navy was that legally their hands were tied, unless war breaks out."

Higgins let the news sink in.

Humph's eyes widened.

"It seems that Lansky somehow let it be known that despite his occupation, he was a patriotic American. He was born in Poland and hated what the Nazis had done there. It turns out that at the beginning of hostilities in Europe, Lansky, powerful gangster and all that, had tried to enlist in the Army. They turned him down because he was forty years old and only five-foot-four."

Humph didn't know how to respond.

"Just goes to show, Humph, people are complicated creatures. We're rarely what we seem to be."

He added that the Navy didn't say they hired Lansky to do their bidding, but it was clear they made some kind of deal with him.

"You can see why such an arrangement can't be publicized."

"Of course," said Humph.

They drank in silence for a long time. Both being thinking men, the suspension of conversation was not unusual or uncomfortable.

Finally, Humph said that what his American soul really needed was a way of joining the fight. He explained that he'd even applied for a job with the FBI fighting the threat of espionage but that he'd been rejected on the grounds that Washington had not approved an expansion in their anti-espionage department.

Higgins was quick to jump in.

"The reason is that, between you and I, their efforts up until now have been nothing short of amateurish."

"But," interrupted Humph, "they nailed eighteen people on espionage charges just recently."

Higgins held up his hand, palm facing Humph, as he'd finished a deep sip of his beer.

"I'll be amazed, Humph, if that case stands up to appeal. These FBI guys are so eager to please Hoover and make him look like America's great protector, they're ready to arrest dandelions for being yellow. They simply don't know what they're doing."

Humph was gratified to know that something was about to be done about the Nazi propaganda machine on U.S. soil, but none of that answered the question he went to Higgins about: What could he do to help?

Higgins didn't have an immediate answer. With apologies, he said:

"Maybe all you can do for now is go to these rallies and find minor charges to bust people on, like insufficient exits in case of fire, or over-capacity attendance, then let the department know and we'll ticket them."

Higgins was probably right, but it irked Humph that an infamous gangster was playing a bigger role in the defense of America than he was.

CHAPTER 9

A few weeks later, Humph knocked on Eve's door. It was the first time he'd visited her new place, on 46th between Eighth and Nineth Avenues. All Broadway theaters were a short walk away. However, Eve had moved there because it was cheap. An old friend had lived there for more than twenty years, and the rent cost not much more than a glamorous dress and a couple of Broadway tickets. Her friend had gone to Hoboken to live with her dying mother. Eve usually didn't sweat money matters, but she'd been out of work for several months.

Eve buzzed him into her second-floor apartment. She waved him to a huge, worse-for-wear easy chair. The flowered wallpaper must have grated on Eve, who was inclined toward bright and flamboyant in her decorating tastes.

"Once I land a role," she explained, having noticed Humph's appraisal of her new place, "I'll only be here to sleep."

"No boyfriend?" asked Humph.

"Nope. And I don't want one until I'm back on track with my career. And," she continued, "until Anke's case is resolved."

Humph asked if she was still visiting the girl at the Tombs. "What a horrid place. I dread just walking in there. How Anke can stand it being there around the clock with all those creeps, and by creeps I mostly mean the guards, I don't know, Dad."

"How is she holding up?" Humph asked.

Eve remained silent for the longest time. Then she got off the tattered, depressingly brown sofa and put a bottle of Scotch on the rickety end table. She went to the kitchen and returned with two glasses and a bowl of ice.

She poured the drinks but still said nothing.

Finally, Humph broke the silence.

"Eve, tell me. What's going on?"

Eve swallowed hard and said:

"Dad, I didn't have the heart to tell you. Anke is dead. She was murdered two weeks ago."

Humph was speechless.

Eve said she went to the detention center the day the murder took place.

"No one would tell me a thing except that my friend wasn't there anymore. I freaked out. I shouted at the guards. I guess I progressed to full-out hysterical. Finally, to shut me up, a matron with more muscle than you pulled me aside and pressed me against the wall of the visiting room.

"'First of all, girlie,' she said. 'Shut up!' She waited a good minute before releasing her grip on me.

"'I don't know the official story, lady, but your girlfriend was murdered. She was stabbed. Her throat was slit as she slept.'

"I was too shocked to utter a sound."

Eve said the guard then volunteered that Anke wasn't the only one. Three men had been murdered the same way overnight.

"The dead guys were being held in the same case as Anke. Then the guard stepped back and stared at me.

"And good riddance, I say," said the guard. "Fucking spies, the lot of them!"

"She then told me to get the hell out and forget my friend."

Eve took a deep swallow of her drink and announced that she'd gone to see the lawyer who was going to get Anke's case dismissed.

"He was in total disbelief. He said he'd been making great headway in preparing his appeal. He had felt confident, totally confident."

Eve said the lawyer then made two phone calls.

"It's true, Eve. What you say is true. They're dead. Murdered."

Humph moved to the sofa and took Eve in his arms.

"It doesn't make sense," he said, "that the prison population would really care at this point about Nazi spies in America. Millions of Americans on the outside don't give a damn. We're not at war."

Humph asked Eve how Anke had been dealing with imprisonment. Eve said she was fine for the first week or two because the lawyer was so positive about getting her off.

"But as time wore on, she got more and more silent. She'd smile at me, but she had retreated inside herself. I wanted to hold her in my arms, but the guards wouldn't allow contact. It was so bad that I stopped going every day. Now I feel so guilty about that."

Humph stood, then raised Eve to her feet.

"You're coming home with me. You need a dose or two of Rebecca."

To Humph's surprise, Eve smiled at the remark.

Humph hailed them a cab. The heavy traffic was a welcome distraction as they rode in near silence.

When they arrived at Tompkins Square, Rebecca had yet to arrive.

"Let's go sit in the park, Dad."

Humph looked at the park across the street, then at Eve.

"First, let's go two blocks that-a-way." He pointed west on East 10ᵗʰ. "I need to get a paper."

He ended up buying two. They returned to the park, each with a paper under their arm.

Humph wanted to see if the Tombs' murders had made the news. Eve joined him in his search.

They both struck out.

"OK," Humph decided. "Let's head home. I have a call to make while we wait for Rebecca."

That call was to his friend, Graham, at the New York World-Telegram.

"I think I have a story for you, my friend. A real good one. The police don't seem to be on it yet, but my girl Eve can attest to the details. If your boys can find out what's behind the story, I'll be forever in your debt, Graham."

After Humph explained, and after Graham briefly spoke to Eve, he told Humph:

"My guys will be headed for the Tombs in just minutes."

"Be assured, Eve," Humph said, "they won't strike out."

Rebecca returned an hour later.

"A long, long, long day," she said in Humph's ear as he hugged her. Even when exhausted, Rebecca could manage a smile.

When she saw Eve on the sofa, she rushed over and took her hands.

"Long story, Rebecca," Humph said.

Over the next hour, Eve explained everything, ending with her Dad's call to the newspaper.

The phone rang a few minutes later. It was a reporter from the paper. He wanted to verify the situation with Anke and the courts and get the contact information for her lawyer. He also wanted to know if Humph had any theories about the three guys who'd been murdered as well. All Humph could offer was that they were convicted at the same trial as Anke.

While Rebecca heated up a dish of pork and beans, Humph took the corner seat of the sofa and went into meditation mode. He didn't call it that, but Eve did. He told himself that if he didn't figure out the connection between the murders, he'd see Higgins first thing the next day.

When Higgins called the Mott Street precinct the next morning, he learned that its chief of detectives was attending a police conference in St. Louis. He then called his friend at the newspaper and learned only that a team of reporters was still investigating. He was disappointed but at the same time delighted that a bunch of reporters, not just one, had been assigned to the case. His friend, Graham, the paper's managing editor, knew that for Humph to be interested in a case meant that it was not small potatoes.

There was only one option left for the moment: a visit to Duffy.

As he headed on foot toward Duffy's walk-up on the Bowery, Humph wondered whether he was starting to show his age as much as his friend. A few blocks later, it occurred to Humph that Duffy resembled his neighborhood, still colorful and vibrant on occasion, but more and more often, mostly drab and sad. Burnt-out people, more and more homelessness, not a lot of laughter on the streets, the new decade wasn't starting out well for the historic neighborhood—just like Duffy.

He still drank like the Irishman he was, but all-nighters were now beyond him. The caustic remarks were fewer and fewer. They had worked together on fewer cases in recent years as well. The last time the two of them had done some serious drinking, Duffy kept coming back to Humph's last big case in which he broke up an international art-theft ring. Duffy played a huge role, sailing to Cuba to defy extradition rules and collar an American conman who was trying to build a fortune with forged or stolen art. Duffy ignored the Cuban state department and enlisted the help of Mexican police to get the thief out of Cuba and on his way to New York for prosecution. On his arrival back in New York, Duffy looked ten years younger than when he left. But it didn't last.

As Humph climbed the stairs to his friend's place, he hoped Duffy would be in decent spirits. He of course wanted to talk about his current investigation, but Duffy was always interested. But if Duffy wanted to pour a drink and sing an Irish tune or two, Humph would enjoy that, too. Duffy was always unpredictable. Humph vaguely felt he should try to adopt that trait as well. Plodding logic had always worked for him, but maybe Rebecca might like a dollop of capriciousness now and then.

As soon as Duffy served him a drink, Humph told him what he had been thinking about as he mounted the stairs.

"Forget it, Humph," Duffy said before Humph had finished elucidating his theory. "That capricious stuff is not in your blood. It can't be manufactured. I was just born that way. I think the first words I ever said to my Mom were, 'Not bloody likely.'"

Duffy was probably right, thought Humph.

"So, boyo, are you working these days?"

Humph meticulously summarized his Nazi-American case. Duffy snapped his fingers a couple of times to hurry him up.

"Well, there was a horrible development. We've launched the appeal of her conviction on espionage charges and got her placed in the Tombs, where the girls can visit her. She's just eighteen, and Eve and Rebecca felt protective of her. Then everything died. I mean, literally and figuratively."

"What's the figure part?" Duffy asked, looking puzzled.

Humph told him what "figuratively" meant.

"If you kill someone figuratively, they're not physically dead. The tragedy in this case is that the girl was stabbed to death in prison. So were three other prisoners, guys, who'd been convicted of espionage at the same trial."

"Who did it?"

"The guards have no idea, or so they say."

Humph added that he'd gone to see the FBI because espionage comes under federal jurisdiction.

"They all but admitted to me that their agents are new to espionage. One of them even said, 'We don't really know what we're doing, but we can't deny that guy in Washington.'"

Duffy looked puzzled.

"That guy in Washington is none other than this nation's wannabe savior, J. Edgar Hoover. He wants to win the war singlehanded."

Humph added:

"I'm sure the girl was innocent. She was killed for nothing. First, she gets raped at this Nazi-friendly camp on Long Island by an instructor. Then she discovers him in Manhattan, under the Manhattan Bridge. He's as drunk as an Irishman and wants to molest her again. The girl grabbed his gun and filled him with holes. Self-defense from the get-go. And even if she'd been forced to attempt some kind of espionage, it was a case of coercion. That's the case we were going to present to the appeals court. But just like the girl—Anke was her name—the case is dead now."

Duffy wanted to know more about the Nazi-American guys. Like Humph, he had read about the huge rally at Madison Square Garden back in the 1930s but knew little to nothing about the Bund's activities since.

"They're taking place all over the country, Duffy. Scares the shit out of me."

Duffy was holding something back. Humph could tell.

To break the silence, Humph said he had a confession to make.

"All this disturbs me so much, Duffy. I feel helpless as an American. I actually tried to enlist in the Army. I'm too old, they said. I then went to the FBI building downtown. They turned me down, too, using the excuse that the anti-espionage department was still in the process of being formed. I wish we'd just declare war and do what's right."

They'd been drinking Scotch. Duffy then pulled out a bottle of Irish whiskey.

"Your heart is in the right place, laddie. I also wish I weren't so ancient."

They drank in silence for some time. Finally, Duffy almost exploded.

"Like you, Humph, I've been tying my guts in knots for a piece of the action against those devils. Did you know that in January those Nazi fornicators bombed the shit out of Dublin, then, just a couple of months ago, did even worse to Belfast? On Easter. Can you believe it? Nine hundred dead, Humph, 1,500 injured.

"I'd like to bayonet every damn American Nazi sympathizer."

Humph felt the same way. Mostly he was glad to see his friend on fire.

They continued talking and drinking, frustrated by not knowing what they could do to eradicate Nazis in America. Then, while quite drunk, Humph alluded to the Mafia. "They could turn out to be our allies," he said, stopping short of explaining his theory.

Duffy was no longer fast on the uptake either.

"Well! Go on!"

Humph slowly explained his unthought-out theory. Several times, he repeated that he hadn't thought things out fully.

"Humph, if there is ever a moment to have foolish faith in heroic action, it's now. Finish your thinking later."

"Lansky," he said. "Meyer Lansky. You remember him from the Lower East Side? A young guy then. A little guy. He scared gangsters with his brain, not his brawn."

Duffy remembered him as if it were yesterday.

"I hear he's the boss of all mob bosses," Duffy said.

Humph then explained what he'd been told to keep a secret. Irish whiskey did that to him.

"At the MSG rally, a lot of the people attending got the crap beaten out of them. And subsequently, at other rallies throughout New Jersey, noggins got hammered. One of my best informants . . ."

"You mean Higgins?" Duffy interrupted.

"Damn you," said Humph. "Yes, Higgins. He said Lansky, who is of course Jewish, has been dispatching his boys to send a message to Nazi sympathizers. And, in the strictest confidence—you hear that, Duff, in the strictest confidence—he told me the U.S. Department of the Navy has made some kind of deal with Lansky giving him a free hand in dealing with these traitors."

Duffy's mouth dropped open.

"The mob has joined the Navy?"

"Rather," said Humph, "the Navy has joined the mob."

CHAPTER 10

A courier from the World-Telegram delivered a large envelope full of newspaper clippings to Humph a week after he got bombed with Duffy, who couldn't stop railing against the Nazi bombing of his cherished Ireland. Humph's last memory filled him with shame. As clear as a bell, he saw himself standing to his full six-foot-two and toasting the Mafia.

Duffy called two days later and asked what Humph remembered of the day. Humph answered that he suspected there were more things to regret than to remember fondly.

"Not much, my friend. Not much. I've got some reading to do about the case. Call you later."

Several hours later, after reading all the clippings Graham had sent, Humph still didn't know what he could do to eradicate the Nazi presence in the country.

Anke's murder had hit him hard. A teenager with no experience of the world indoctrinated by people willing to murder and promote hatred at every opportunity, she didn't stand a chance at the Long Island camp.

Rebecca had the day off, and her preferred form of relaxation was to cook Puerto Rican dishes. She'd been at it all afternoon. Some of the dishes benefitted from slow cooking and tons of piquant preparation. That morning, she'd happily gone all the way to Spanish Harlem to shop for ingredients. With the advent of air travel, migration from Puerto Rico was exploding. Rebecca was hoping some of them would settle in Lower Manhattan and open a market or two. For the moment, they had congregated in the Bronx and Harlem.

That evening, Humph sat down to a dinner of chicken and potato stew to which Rebecca had added a cup of sofrito, a sauteed mixture of onions, garlic, peppers and whatever else the cook felt inspired to add.

Humph had grown to love every single dish from Rebecca's Puerto Rican repertoire. He was a man of appetites—food being one, beautiful women being another—and as big an appetite as was justice, be it for a vagrant being pushed aside on the sidewalk by a man in a suit, or Nazis infiltrating America.

His other big appetite was baseball. Born in Manhattan, he was a Yankees fan. The week before, they'd defeated the Brooklyn Dodgers in what had just been dubbed the Subway Series, winning the series four games to one. Maybe life wasn't so bad after all, Humph decided while celebrating the victory with Duffy, who had no interest whatsoever in this boring American game.

"But, Humph, if I did give a damn about the World Series, I would have rooted for Brooklyn."

"And why would that be?"

"Because people in Brooklyn don't wear expensive suits. They're real people."

Rebecca had been busy dishing out a second serving and hadn't noticed her husband's departure to Ebbets Field.

When she returned to the table, Rebecca asked Humph point-blank:

"Still thinking about poor Anke, aren't you?"

Humph turned to her and nodded.

He offered no words. Rebecca leaned closer to him over the table.

"I've been thinking. Maybe my idea is stupid. The one thing I know is that you want to, you need to, be involved in the fight against these American Nazis. So, this morning, while I sat on a bench across from the market listening to bomba tunes . . ."

The term drew a blank look from Humph.

"It's an African-Puerto Rican style of music. It goes back a long way. I grew up with it."

"We should get a record," Humph said. "I could use something that celebrates being alive."

Rebecca loved his answer.

"We will, for sure. But in the meantime, I got this idea while listening this morning. Tell me what you think.

"How good or how bad is your German?"

Humph thought for a moment, then said that being at the Nazi camp made him realize he remembered more German that he thought he knew.

"The accent came back. That's what surprised me. Nobody called me out on my German."

Rebecca said her idea might mean taking some kind of German refresher course.

"Do you have time for that?"

"You know damn well that I haven't had a big case in a dog's age."

"Good, Humph. Here's my idea, cockamamie or not. You can be honest, but for now just listen.

"In Anke's honor, why don't you try offering yourself

to be an instructor of some kind at the camp? It will make it possible to meet other girls who are being beaten, brainwashed and sexually abused."

Humph didn't answer.

"Besides," Rebecca added, "all these girls may be of German parents, but do they all speak fluent German? I doubt it. If the instructors at the camp find your German lacking, they will also understand that it's normal for someone who has lived his whole life in America."

Humph was clearly intrigued by her idea.

"Tell me more," he said.

Rebecca knew that Humph wouldn't have responded that way if he'd thought her idea was ludicrous. He would have politely changed the subject.

Rebecca elaborated on her idea. She said that if he ever wanted to get back at the Bund, he'd have to somehow infiltrate the camp. He'd have to become an instructor. She said that was the only way he could learn whether the abuse of young women was common. How many got humiliated, beaten and even raped?

Humph nodded.

Rebecca continued:

"Remember, Humph, that the camp's purpose is to train spies. If you worked there, you could find out how they do that. In my thoughts, I pictured you dismantling their whole indoctrination program."

Humph smiled broadly.

"Am I your superhero? What's that new cartoon? Yeah, Superman."

"Absolutely. You're my Superman," Rebecca answered, laughing.

Humph reached across the table and lifted her up, plunking her down on his lap.

"You're brilliant as well as beautiful. We'll do the dishes tomorrow."

The next morning, Humph awoke, excited by Rebecca's idea. He phoned Duffy.

"I'm on my way, no matter what state you're in."

As usual, he stopped at the newsstand to get the morning papers. The main war story was that the Germans, while still advancing on the Russian giant, were awaiting frosts to end the rains that muddied the route for tanks.

He wanted to get his hands dirty, right there in America.

It all seemed somehow unreal to Humph. He imagined millions of Americans felt the same way. The unreality made the future all the more frightening.

Newspapers in hand, he made his way back to Duffy's Celtic cave in the Bowery. He was eager to hear Duffy's reaction to Rebecca's idea. He was glad to see that his friend hadn't started drinking yet. In fact, Duffy listened in respectful silence until Humph finished explaining. Humph suspected it wasn't out of respect for him but rather for his devastatingly sensual lass, Rebecca.

When Humph went silent, Duffy rose, grabbed two glasses with one hand and proceeded to fill them halfway with whiskey.

As he sat back on the sofa, he said:

"To summarize, me boyo, Rebecca says we should get to know members of the Bund, the ordinary American kind, the ones who proved their devotion to Hitler and fascists everywhere years ago by giving birth to bright-eyed Yankee kids brought up to respect their parents and then respect their passions and principles."

"Succinctly stated, Duff. However, the question now is how do we meet them?"

Duffy told Humph to hold his horses. He disappeared into his bedroom and returned with some pamphlets and other papers.

"We got these at Camp Siegfried, remember? I'd bet the odds are pretty good we'll find the address of the Bund headquarters somewhere in these documents."

After a couple of minutes, Humph was the one who spotted it.

"It's here in Manhattan, in an area called Yorkville. The address is 178 East 85th Street. It's right near Third Avenue, so there'll be no Irish labor involved in getting there."

"When you get sarcastic like that, little man, it means your glass is empty. You can bloody well pour your own this time."

An hour later, the pair headed north on the Third Avenue train. They arrived at what Duffy called Nazi Headquarters in no time at all.

"I forgot," said Duff. "What are we going to do here?"

"What else, Duffy? I'm going to apply for a job to work at Camp Siegfried. I've always wanted to teach."

"And what about me?" Duffy said.

Duffy spoke no German, and probably wouldn't want to even if he could. Bombing Dublin on Easter was beyond forgiving.

"Are you any good with your hands, Duffy?"

The Irishman replied by raising both hands simultaneously, suggesting being able to drink right- or lefthanded.

"You can be insufferable."

Duffy laughed as if he enjoyed being insufferable.

Humph put a meaty hand on each of Duffy's shoulders.

"Listen. From our first visit, especially the rescue of Anke, you must remember the camp has tennis courts, kayaks, row boats and so on. They surely need repairs now and then. If not, you can fake it. And all those hiking trails, they have to be maintained, right?"

Duffy was getting the idea.

"I absolutely must become an instructor of some kind. Obviously I'm not going to get a job teaching Nazi propaganda or espionage techniques, but I can attend class so that when I take these kids out to hike, swim, whatever,

I can reinforce what they've been learning that day in class. Or at least that's the line I'm going to give the instructors. I have enough German for that."

Duffy nodded. "Doable," he said.

"After a few weeks," continued Humph, "the kids, especially the girls, might start trusting me enough to open up about whatever bad stuff is going on, you know, the kinds of things Anke had to endure, the assaults, the beatings, the humiliation. We won't be able to nail anyone for espionage against the United States, but rape is rape. I've talked to Higgins about this, and he shook my hand and said, 'Call and I'll come a-runnin'.'"

He said getting a conviction or two of that kind could open the door to shutting down the camp and giving the Bund a legal black eye.

Signing up at the Bund headquarters seemed to be a simple affair: name; address; phone, if any; reason for joining, which Humph answered with "our shared beliefs"; country of birth. Humph wondered what their response would be if he cited a Negro nation in Africa.

Unlike Humph, Duffy couldn't forge a German-like accent. In fact, he cited Ireland as his place of birth. However, in the brief interview with the front-desk receptionist, a man, he explained that in recent years, his good friend who was accompanying him, Herr Barstal, had won him over to ideas championed by the Bund.

The clerk seemingly accepted the explanation.

"It is essential that we, as a group, expand in numbers to get the word out to as many Americans as possible before the next elections," he said.

He then asked the two men to wait a few moments.

When the man returned not a couple of minutes later but fifteen minutes later, the bottom fell out of Humph's plan.

The desk clerk had two neatly dressed but overly muscled security men with him.

"I have just made an unfortunate discovery, gentlemen. The two of you have been recognized for what you are. You are infiltrators."

Humph was able to keep a deadpan face, but Duffy's feigned incredulity was halfway comical. Humph averted his eyes from his friend. They met those of the officious desk clerk.

"You have been recognized as the man who manipulated his way to talk to our young women campers. Then you and your friend here were observed hurrying to remove her from the confines of Camp Siegfried. In America or in Germany, that's called kidnapping."

"Germans are supposed to be so studious," replied Humph. "I assumed they had much better memories for facts. We kidnapped no one. We rescued her because your boys were guilty of abusing a young teenage girl. Here in America, that is called sexual assault of the worst kind."

If looks could kill, neither Humph nor Duffy would have ever walked out of there.

The muscle boys shuffled their feet awaiting the boss's word. Humph turned suddenly toward the entrance. Duffy didn't wait to be asked to follow.

Once out on Third Avenue, Duffy caught up to Humph and said, "I swear, Humph, if you catch me drinking a German beer again, you have my permission to send me to meet my maker."

Once they were back on the El train, Duffy could see how disappointed Humph was that his plan had been foiled at the outset. "What next?"

"I need to see Higgins," he answered. He was also thinking that Rebecca would be sorely disappointed by his misfortune.

When they arrived at the precinct, they learned that the chief of detectives was locked in a meeting. Because Higgins's office was full, the two private eyes would have to wait downstairs and enjoy a bird's-eye view of the parade of oddballs and misfortunates who had to see the desk sergeant.

After almost half an hour, Duffy suggested they leave a message with the desk sergeant and wait at the nearby cop's bar. Humph didn't want to.

"You go, Duff, and I'll call you when Higgins is available."

"You're a good man, Humph. While I'm there, know that I'll be trying to convince the barkeep to cease selling German beer."

As he left, Humph wondered what Duffy was going to do with the case of German beer that sat on the floor behind his corner easy chair. Would it go down the toilet or down his gullet? He could hear his friend now: "Waste not, want not."

After an hour-long wait, Higgins was free. Immediately, he could tell the big man was unhappy.

"Our glorious plan for saving young women and saving America . . ." Humph paused.

Higgins had never seen him so emotional. Not much in this world knocked a cop of more than twenty years out of the saddle. Higgins had been watching a slew of westerns to close the last gaps in his knowledge of American lore and mentality. It would be useful in interrogating, he thought. The fact was, he had adored westerns since childhood in Scotland. However, it was a young companion at university in Edinburgh who had nailed the reason for the appeal of westerns, at least to a non-American. He was from the tiny nation of Holland.

"Space," the young man said.

"You mean wide-open spaces and all that?" Higgins replied.

"Exactly. Exactly what doesn't exist in Europe."

Higgins came back to the present. His mental absence hadn't been noted. Humph was clearly derailed. Had he begun to regard young Anke as a daughter of sorts?

Gently, Higgins insisted on knowing what had happened on the Upper East Side, at the Bund headquarters.

As if reading from a constable's notebook, Humph recounted exactly what had taken place.

When he finished, Higgins looked at him for some time. Humph said nothing.

"That is indeed a disappointment, my friend. But it's not your fault."

"In fact," he continued, "it makes me all the more want to trample through their garden, so to speak. Their antagonism toward you proves how close the removal of dear Anke hit home."

Finally, Humph opened up.

"What I most wanted, whether they made me an instructor or not, was access to all the girls there. At the very least, I wanted a list of their names and addresses here in New York. In the end, I got zero."

Higgins shuffled papers, then finally spoke to Humph.

"I'm sure I can do something about that. I'll be in touch, my friend."

CHAPTER 11

AS expected, Rebecca was disappointed. She even threw a sofa cushion all the way into the kitchen. Because he didn't have the words to respond immediately to the outburst, as expected as it was, Humph got up and retrieved the cushion. He held it on his lap rather than place it next to Rebecca.

He pulled her to him.

"I don't know when, Rebecca, but we will honor Anke's memory in time. That's what I was hoping to move toward today, but the Nazi bastards caught me. It's not over, not by a long shot."

Just at that moment, the phone rang. Rebecca wasn't going to answer it. Humph did on the sixth ring. The caller was insistent.

"Humph, it's Higgins. I have a plan. See me tomorrow."

Humph was desperate to know what it was, but Higgins had gone.

The next day took its damn old time to arrive.

Humph showed up early at the precinct.

The flatfoots were learning their day's assignments from the duty sergeant. It was a routine so well known to Humph he almost felt that all was well.

Finally, Humph was told he could go up to Higgins's office. When he got there, there were four uniformed cops in his office but no Higgins. Was this some kind of uniform-cop revolt?

A moment later, a hand clapped him on the back. Higgins had approached silently. He had been in the captain's office down the hall.

"Come in, Humph. I'm about to give them their marching orders. I'll be going with them. You're welcome to come along for the ride."

Humph still had no idea what Higgins was up to, but he eagerly followed.

Higgins addressed the four officers.

"A-hunting we shall go. Time to go camping, boys. See you all at Camp Siegfried."

Humph was happy his friend stopped short of singing the nursery rhyme *hi ho the derry-o, a-hunting we shall go.*

He was even happier once in the patrol car when Higgins began explaining his plan. He and Higgins sat in the back seat. The chief of detectives got his own driver.

It turned out that the detective's plan first required a stop at the Bund's Upper East Side headquarters.

With the towering Humph at his side, he walked up to the main desk, flashed his badge and demanded to see a list of members and their dependents, in short, anyone who had attended the camp that year. The clerk hesitated for a moment, and an officious-looking man in a suit appeared out of nowhere.

He had overhead the request from Higgins.

"No no no," he ordered. Humph's ears instantly heard that as, "Nein nein nein!"

The man insisted that the information on Bund members was private.

Higgins walked to within inches of him and said, "Yes yes yes." He and the German-speaker locked eyes.

The Bund honcho noticed Humph by the information counter.

"You!" He pointed at Humph. "I threw you out just the other day."

Higgins edged even closer to the man and said, "This time, he's with me."

The man lowered his voice and backed up a little.

"This is an official police request. Failure to hand over the pages willingly will result in your office, your headquarters for all of New York, being padlocked. God knows what the publicity will be like."

The last remark hung in the air. It had hit home. The Bund officer acquiesced. Humph was sure the little bow he gave Higgins was a sarcastic gesture.

Twenty minutes later, Humph carried a large carton of print-outs down to the patrol car.

As they arrived on the street, Higgins quipped:

"I knew you'd be yourself this morning."

Once in the back seat, Humph maneuvered the box between them. Higgins signaled to the driver to get underway.

"Why did you want all these names and addresses, Higgins?"

"Well, Humph, since we have no evidence of a crime at the moment, we can't question the girls at the camp. However, they've got to come home soon. Summer's over and the weather is going to turn. Once they're home with mommy and daddy, we can approach the parents and see which of them are patriotic enough to entertain our theories about what goes on there, citing Anke's case. If the parents give us permission to talk to the girls and we're thorough enough, I have a good feeling that we'll strike gold, as ugly as it may be."

"My hat's off to you, Higgins."

They rode in silence for some time. Humph found himself thinking of Anke.

"You know, Higgins, I'm sure more than a couple of the girls will remember Anke, or will at least have heard of her fate. Odds are they'll shorten our search by a lot."

"Exactly, Humph. My thought as well." Then, looking directly at Humph, he wondered: "I guess it would be asking too much to hope that one of the girls will spill the beans today."

Higgins laughed. "For such a gloomy Gus, you're still an eternal optimist."

The traffic was bad everywhere. Eventually, they made it to the Triborough Bridge to get off Manhattan. The bridge merged with the Grand Central Parkway, where traffic miraculously lessened. However, it wasn't easy finding the hamlet of Yaphank, Long Island, the proud home of Camp Siegfried.

When they arrived at the camp entrance, Higgins was relieved to see his officers could also navigate well.

With Higgins at the head, they made their way to the entrance. The clerk was young and not about to challenge the police. At the head office, Higgins announced his intention to interview all girls who knew of Anke. The clerk at the counter feigned ignorance of the name or the idea of anyone being abused at the camp. Higgins instructed an officer to search the desk for logbooks and membership information for the young ladies present. To Humph's surprise, Higgins had already obtained a search warrant from a New York judge. It was valid anywhere in the state, he told the counter clerk who was about to object again.

When the police announced they wanted to interview the girls, refusal was fast in coming. Higgins had anticipated that, and it was for that reason he had obtained their records from Bund headquarters.

"Why did we bother?" asked Humph.

"Simply put, my friend, to put the fear of God in them. The camp's days are numbered, I assure you."

Before heading back to New York, Higgins and his boys stood on the beach, enjoying the ocean breeze, the rhythmic waves and the shrieks of young American teenagers enjoying a summer far from the concrete of Manhattan.

What they couldn't see from the beach were young children, some as young as six, doing all the labor around the camp. The Bund didn't want to hire outsiders to do such work and possibly spy on them. The children had no choice but to do as they were told, just as they had no choice about watching Nazi propaganda films and learning Nazi songs and salutes.

On the way home, Higgins intimated to Humph that camps like that would not survive to the end of the year.

"Details?"

"Not allowed to tell you yet. Let's just say America is waking up. In the meantime, let's round up these Nazi rapists and spies."

When Humph got home, he was elated. To add to his joy, Eve showed up with Rebecca half an hour later.

Eve wanted in on the interrogation of the girls.

"It's not an interrogation, Eve," said Humph. "They're guilty of nothing. All we want is information and corroboration. We have to be gentle. If they got mistreated at camp, it was without doubt the worst experience of their life. Make them your friends."

Humph had already talked to Higgins about using Eve, or any other woman, to do the questioning. He agreed.

Several weeks later, before they ever got to the questioning of the women, the State Department stepped in. They closed the camp and shut down the Bund. Their actions were accompanied by a string of arrests of suspected spies. The federal rulings resulted in nationwide closings of pro-Nazi groups.

Despite the closing of the camps, Higgins decided to pursue the questioning of the girls in the hope of discovering evidence that might lead to charges against the camp instructors, but the case soon found itself on the backburner in the face of the ongoing crime in the city. Already, the NYPD was losing men to the armed forces. Higgins worried that the department might soon find itself seriously short of the manpower it needed. Crime was showing no sign of abating.

At the same time, to the government's surprise and delight, the First Amendment supporters of the Nazi and fascist movements in the country faded into the woodwork. The war in Europe was growing more terrifying for the free world by the day. According to the polls, Americans were doing an about-face. Enlistment numbers were soaring. Editorial pages suddenly recognized that America was part of the world.

However, his war against Camp Siegfried having been dealt with all of a sudden, Humph felt part of nothing.

CHAPTER 12

THE gray skies of December echoed Humph's mood. Newspaper articles describing the deaths of millions during Operation Barbarossa, the German attack on Russia, fit right into the mood. Mankind was comprised of madmen. There was no other conclusion, he thought.

God bless Broadway. It still brought light to New Yorkers. As World War II approached, a dozen Broadway dramas addressed the rise of Nazism in Europe and the issue of American non-intervention. Rebecca was working non-stop as a result. She admitted one evening that of late, she preferred being on just off Seventh Avenue than at home in Tompkins Square. A big man like her husband could cast an enormous pall over home life. Nobody visited, not even Humph's buddy, Duffy. And his "daughter", Eve, had opted to meet Rebecca for coffee or lunch in Midtown rather than at her home.

Humph still went out for the morning papers, more out of habit than enthusiasm. His mood may have dampened his natural curiosity, but none of the stories suggested cases for him to investigate. Then a letter appeared in the mailbox. The name of the sender meant nothing, but part of the return address did: Andover, New Jersey.

Humph remembered that there was a Bund camp there, just like the Siegfried camp on Long Island.

The letter was from a man who claimed to be young. He said his family belonged to the Bund. He and his younger sister, age seventeen, had been sent to the Bund's summer camp in Andover. The young man said his sister had been raped by an instructor. The camp sent her home because "she had become too neurotic" to follow through with her studies. In parenthesis, the writer of the letter wrote that those studies focused on Nazi beliefs.

"My sister, whom I love so much, has been a vegetable since she was returned home. I am desperate for help. I read about the case you solved with regard to a similar case in Long Island recently. Please, sir, reply at your earliest convenience."

He signed the letter as Dieter Schmidt.

Humph took the letter to Higgins that afternoon.

"It's never too late to prosecute," the chief of detectives said. "The German American Bund has been shuttered, but its past is still fair game."

For almost an hour, they discussed ways of approaching the Andover case. Was the young man's letter enough to get a search warrant for his parents' home? Could they talk to the victim, only seventeen, without the consent of parents? What did they need to know for the girl's claims to stand up in court? Could they prove rape so long after the fact? Would the traumatized girl even talk to them? Would they be obliged to involve New Jersey cops?

With one exception, Higgins said he'd have to lay the groundwork.

"What I'd like you to do, Humph, is talk to Eve. She was passionate about the Anke tragedy, and you told me she was so upset by her murder in prison that she ceased functioning for weeks. Maybe—tell me what you think—if she can be the one who talks to the victim on our behalf, Eve might become herself again. We need a woman to talk to her."

As soon as Humph returned to Tompkins Square, he talked to Rebecca, who took it upon herself to call Eve. Eve showed up at their home within an hour.

Humph summarized the letter young Dieter Schmidt had sent him. He had to give the physical letter to Higgins that morning. He then described the conversation he and Higgins had, the conditions that would have to be met to obtain a useful and informative interview with the girl and her family.

"Higgins will be there. I'll be there. But we need someone like you, Eve, to try to get the poor girl to open up about what happened and who was responsible. From what her brother told me, she is in such a bad way that she may refuse to talk at all."

There was no answer from Eve.

Finally, Humph said:

"I know how you became a real friend to Anke. She valued you in the end. And I know how much you suffered when Anke was murdered. Higgins knows, too. In fact, he was the one who suggested to me that it might do you, and the case, good to try to win this Jersey girl's trust, woman to woman."

Eve walked toward her "dad", who was seated in an easy chair. She knelt down and, with both hands, took Humph's huge left hand.

"I'll try, Dad. Maybe we can give her back a life."

Humph lifted her to her feet and hugged her tightly.

When Eve eventually pushed away from his chest, she said to Rebecca: "Any Scotch left?"

While Rebecca poured a double for Eve, Humph called Higgins at home with the good news.

Higgins said almost everything was in place for their invasion of New Jersey.

"You and Eve, can you be ready to leave around noon tomorrow?"

Before Higgins's patrol car arrived the next morning, Humph phoned the exchange for Andover and asked for the number for a Mr. Schmidt on Lakeview Avenue. He then asked Rebecca to make the call.

"Just ask for Dieter. If asked, say you represent an encyclopedia company or something like that."

A woman answered. Dieter came on the line a moment later. Rebecca immediately passed the phone to her husband. After introducing himself, Humph explained:

"This is late notice, Dieter, but unavoidable. We'll be arriving in an hour or ninety minutes."

"Who is 'we'?" the young man asked.

"The police, a doctor and a woman we'd like to have talk to your sister."

"I don't know how to thank you."

"Who is home right now? You, your sister, who else?"

"Just my mom. She answered the phone."

"OK. Just don't say anything about our visit. Say the call was from a salesperson."

Humph couldn't help but wonder why Dieter was not at work. He didn't know how old he was, but his voice was not that of a teenager. When he mentioned that to Eve, who still remembered her teenage years, during which she functioned as an adult, a burlesque performer and a stripper, she said:

"And what, pray tell, does a teenager sound like?"

"Point taken," said Humph.

When they arrived, Higgins led the way up the three steps to the front door of a comfortable, large, two-story house set on a spacious lawn with more than a dozen trees.

Hazel Schmidt, Dieter's mother, met them at the door. A young man in his early twenties, who Humph assumed was Dieter, was right behind her.

"Mrs. Schmidt," said Higgins, "I represent the NYPD. We have questions to ask you, your son, Dieter and your daughter, Christa."

"New York? You're from New York? You don't have jurisdiction here!"

"If you'd care to read them," Higgins replied in a commanding tone, "I have papers saying we do."

Before Mrs. Schmidt had time to look at the documents, Higgins had brushed by her. His team followed.

He introduced himself to Dieter.

"Thanks for contacting us. Where is your sister's room?"

Dieter led them all upstairs. He entered first, sat down on the side of the bed, took his sister's hand and softly said, "All these people are here to help. They've already helped a girl who had the same thing happen at a Siegfried camp in New York."

At that point, the New York medical examiner quietly slipped into the room. Higgins introduced him.

The doctor sat next to Christa.

"Did a man do something to you?"

Christa stared at him for a minute, then nodded.

"May I examine you? It won't hurt."

The doctor's face was gentle, his voice soft. The girl nodded again.

Eve stepped in and knelt by the bed. She took Christa's hand and leaned close to Christa's face.

Christa stared back. Her look was penetrating. Eve smiled slightly.

In the time the girl took to absorb Eve's presence, the doctor had completed her examination and pulled down her nightgown.

The doctor motioned Higgins to leave the room. Outside, he told the detective that there were still signs of bruising in the vaginal area as well as on her rib cage.

"The girl has definitely been abused."

Higgins thanked him and told him he could wait in the car if he wished.

When he returned to the room, Eve was already at Christa's bedside. Higgins withdrew to let her build some kind of relationship. He wouldn't press for answers that day.

At first the mother denied any knowledge of a Nazi organization. She swore her husband was red-white-and-blue to his very core. She said she voted Republican and was church-going.

"Check my voting record, for heaven's sake. We're all Americans in the township. Deep-down Americans."

She was approaching hysteria at the suggestion she was anything but.

A search of the home turned up letters with Nazi-like mentions. More importantly, it turned up documents verifying their membership in the Bund.

Not long after, Mr. Schmidt, the father, burst through the door. He was furious. The only thing that could have set him off was the sight of the cop car out front.

"We don't need any cops here. We take care of our own. Now get the hell out!"

Higgins calmly showed him the warrant.

"If you have any damn questions, you can ask me. Leave my family alone."

"Read the warrant," said Higgins. "It gives us the right to search the premises."

Pacing angrily, Mr. Schmidt heard the sound of the door to his daughter's room opening.

"You have no damn right to talk to my children!"

"We have your wife's permission," said Higgins.

"Hazel," he hollered. "Get down here instantly!"

She was already coming down the stairs by the time her husband finished shouting.

Since the police had arrived, she'd struck everyone as being a kindly, well-mannered woman. However, Higgins and Humph were surprised and impressed at how calmly and steadily she returned her husband's scowl.

"How could you?" he demanded.

"How could I what?" Hazel replied, as steady as a rock. "Our daughter needs help, but you're too rabid to see that. That stupid camp of yours, I wish I'd never heard of it."

Waving his finger in her face, Mr. Schmidt said, "Have you forgotten, woman, that you are a signed-up Bund member?"

"What does that have to do with anything? Our daughter was abused by your arrogant Bund buddies. What is more important to you, them or your daughter?"

"Sacrifices have to be made in times like these."

For the first time, his wife lost control.

"What kind of animal are you? You talk of sacrifice for the cause while your own flesh and blood is in agony! May God burn a damn swastika on your forehead for all to see until your dying day. You bastard! Get out of this house. Right now!" She started pounding his chest.

Humph privately applauded her at the same moment he thrust his huge frame between the couple.

As he moved Schmidt to the other side of the room, his eye caught the eyes of young Dieter, frozen on the stairs. He seemed to be shaking.

He didn't see Eve or the doctor. Thank goodness they had ignored the screaming and stayed with Christa in her room.

Eve was later to tell him that they had heard every word of the scream. Christa clutched Eve's arm as tears rolled down her face.

"It was our first connection," she told Humph. "I have a feeling this wasn't the first time she'd heard her father raise his voice."

Higgins told Schmidt to calm down or face arrest.

"On what damned charge, you idiot?" The man was a tinderbox who respected no authority but his own.

"That does it," said Higgins. Turning to a constable, he ordered: "Cuff him and take him to the kitchen."

After going upstairs to check on how Eve and the doctor were faring, he told them to let Christa in peace when they felt she'd had enough. The doctor took Higgins to the hall and whispered, "The girl trusts Eve. I think it would be most profitable if I left them alone."

Higgins was delighted. Knowing the girl's state when they arrived, he had expected no real progress so soon.

"Your girl has quite the touch," he told Humph.

In an uncharacteristically soft voice, Humph replied simply that Eve knew what Christa's kind of pain was.

Higgins and Humph then entered the kitchen and sat at the table facing Mr. Schmidt.

What followed was a detailed inquiry into his involvement in the Bund and its activities, locally and, as the case may be, in New York. They also learned he was born in the U.S. of near-noble German stock, or so he claimed. He said the Bund afforded him the only outlet for denouncing Jews, socialists and "cursed exponents of rights for those brown people who pretend to be Americans".

Higgins glanced sideways at Humph. Humph understood the warning. It translated as: "Schmidt deserves to have the crap beaten out of him, but I'm sure Rebecca would rather see him in jail. Hands off!"

Schmidt's wife had already said she was Republican through and through, but the longer Higgins and Humph questioned Schmidt, the more it seemed his heart lay with more radical right-wing interests.

It was clear that Schmidt was arrogant, and pedantic, by nature. Despite being handcuffed at his own kitchen table, he launched himself into a lecture about the only sane course a true American could follow politically. He name-dropped someone called Gerald Smith. Neither Humph nor Higgins had heard of him. Schmidt explained that the man was one of democracy's greatest political organizers in the fight against FDR, Jews and colored people, and excessive government involvement in the lives of Americans.

"Gentlemen," said Schmidt, in full-lecture mode, "after aligning himself with international fascists, this God-fearing man even reached out to Adolph Hitler himself for guidance."

Humph and Higgins simultaneously felt a chill. They were dealing with a madman, an all-American madman, a racist member of the Old Guard, the old right, the core of deep Republican belief.

They had enough information to get Schmidt tagged in their records as a possible anti-American fascist and face a charge of domestic abuse. That charge seldom led anywhere, but at least the bastard would have a record.

Higgins had him put in a patrol car.

Eve requested that she be allowed to stay another day with Christa. Her mom, Hazel, agreed. Humph and Higgins said "yes" and headed back to New York.

In the comfort of his Tompkins Square home, Humph recounted every detail to Rebecca, including Schmidt's hatred of non-whites. "It's a common denominator for far-right-wingers, it seems."

Rebecca didn't even bother to comment.

"I'm so proud of Eve," she said.

Humph hugged her. The embrace was for both women.

Two days later, Eve called Humph.

"Christa gave me the name of the man who raped her. He had been a camp instructor. He lives not far from

Andover. I've got the address. She knew it because the instructor asked her to visit him at his home."

Humph called Higgins immediately.

Warrant in hand, he returned to New Jersey to affect the arrest of a young man who at first denied ever having gone to the camp. Higgins knew he would not last long under interrogation.

The next evening, Higgins, Duff and Humph met at the police pub. They toasted the removal of the last Nazi seed in the New York area. As they sipped, words grew fewer. Humph ordered another round in the hope of reviving conversation.

Just as the waiter was placing the drinks on the table in front of them, a radio was turned to full volume.

"I repeat," the announcer said, "at 7:55 a.m., the Japanese attacked Pearl Harbor." The pub went silent.

Humph said to no one in particular, "We're at war."

CHAPTER 13

THE next morning, Humph and Rebecca had their worst argument.

Rebecca not only said no to his idea, but she also said she'd never talk to him again if he proceeded.

Humph answered:

"I'm not a man, I'm not an American, if I don't."

An hour later, Humph stood in front of the military recruiting office on Whitehall Street in Lower Manhattan. It was a relatively short walk from Tompkins Square.

Upset by the argument with Rebecca, he swallowed deeply and entered.

It was a short visit.

"We salute your patriotism, sir, but soldiering is for young men. In the very near future, there will be endless volunteer opportunities, from selling bonds to knitting socks for soldiers." The soldier made the comment as the two men shook hands. Humph's hand dwarfed his. Humph laughed, imagining needles in his fingers.

The FBI had already refused Humph. Time to face facts, he guessed. At least Rebecca would be happy with the morning's rejection.

Higgins was his next stop.

When Humph stepped into his office, Higgins noticed and immediately turned back to face the detective he had been chatting with. "Later," said Higgins, dismissing the man.

"How's your day been so far?" he asked Humph, while pointing him to the chair in front of his desk.

"Miserable on all fronts."

He briefly recounted the argument with Rebecca over breakfast, their worst ever.

"She said she'd leave me if I enlisted in the Army. Fortunately, the Army didn't want me either. I feel so useless."

Higgins said there were other things he could do.

"What? I sure don't know. I told you I already tried getting on with the FBI. I wanted to investigate spies, traitors, you know. All that. I was out the door in ten minutes."

Higgins waited, but Humph had shut down. He had never been one to feel sorry for himself or complain frivolously.

Finally, Higgins said he couldn't offer anything official at the moment but said the country's entry into the war was already causing changes at the NYPD.

"We're losing officers at an alarming rate. They're signing up as soldiers. If only criminals would do the same, but they're not."

Humph suddenly sat up straight in his chair.

"And another thing," Higgins said. "Now that war

is on, the State Department isn't holding me on a tight leash anymore. They need all-out help from everybody, including us."

He admitted that the NYPD had been conducting some minor investigations into potential traitors.

"Now they want us to step up our efforts. I'm thinking of creating a special force of some kind. For now, I have no idea what form that will take. I know what the State Department is concerned about, and the FBI has been instructed to focus on those areas, but as cops we have our ears to the ground constantly. We know what the local grocer has observed, we know what the punks on the street are yakking about. The FBI doesn't. I can at least tell you that one of the major areas of concern for the government right now is major ports, and we're the biggest."

Humph felt his feet were on solid ground again.

Higgins said he couldn't reveal more at the moment.

"But the time will come when I can let you in the door. There are some surprising things in the works."

Humph nodded, then added:

"Change of subject. Have you heard anything from Eve of late?"

Higgins slapped his desktop hard.

"By God, yes, Humph. What a girl."

Humph had tried to contact her, but she never seemed to be home.

Higgins recapped.

"Now that we have that closet Nazi, that Schmidt asshole, charged, even though he's out on bail, we got a restraining order. He can't go anywhere near his house or family members."

Humph was relieved. He had detested Schmidt from the instant he met him.

"But the big news," added Higgins, "was that the girl, his daughter, finally opened up to your Eve, just the way

Anke once did. She named her abuser, the camp instructor, and recounted how her damned father told the instructor he had nothing to worry about. In Christa's hearing, he actually said he would straighten out his daughter about what was important in these trying times."

Humph interrupted. "That explains why he has been totally unsupportive about Christa. He considers her complaining about being raped as being anti-Nazi. This is beyond belief, Higgins."

Higgins agreed. The NYPD was going to investigate him to the fullest extent of the law.

"Since we shut down the Bund, Nazi sympathizers have been disappearing into the woods, in some cases, and in others, putting our flag on their verandahs to show they're model citizens."

"I'd give anything to go after Schmidt," said Humph.

"No, my friend. I've already got two men on the case."

As Humph's heart was sinking again, Higgins added that he would soon have something "to dig your teeth into".

Humph stood, bent down and shook his hand. Without saying a word, he left.

A Bowery visit suddenly appeared on Humph's mental list.

At the corner of Bowery and Broom Street, just moments before Humph's arrival, a horse-drawn milk delivery wagon had been hit by a car. The horse wasn't yet dead, but his left front leg and hip were mangled by the impact. He would have to be put down. The driver of the wagon lay on the street, moaning. The driver of the car complained loudly to anyone who would listen that "that damned wagon ignored a red light". A bystander told him to shut up. "I saw what happened, you bastard."

Humph liked horses. Every year, fewer and fewer were being used for deliveries. If only, Humph thought, they could remove them from service at Central Park.

Briefly, in his days as an NYPD patrolman, he became part of their mounted squad, which specialized in crowd control at demonstrations and riots. He regretted having been assigned to other duties at a downtown precinct.

When he got to Duffy's place, he had shaken off the sad scene.

He didn't want to get drunk with his friend. His major concern was making peace with Rebecca, who said she'd be working late that evening. As he mounted the stairs, he found himself thinking that he could have a few drinks, then have time to sober up for the late arrival of his wife.

It was no surprise, but it was obvious from the moment Duffy let him in the door that he'd been drinking.

As Humph sat, Duffy shrugged and said, "It's past noon, after all."

"Pour," Humph ordered.

After consuming half a tumbler of Irish whiskey, Humph recounted his day. Duffy commiserated about the sad morning with Rebecca and the outrage of his rejection by the recruiting office, and added the opinion that the milk wagon driver was probably Irish. However, the subject he returned to the instant Humph grew silent was the world "Higgy" seemed to be opening to them.

"Us?" queried Humph.

"Well, yes. You and I are a team. No? If he suggests a new future for you, he's including me."

"Pour!"

Duffy complied with a grin.

Finally, Humph asked Duffy why Higgins would include him.

"The docks, you dolt!"

"What about the docks? Sure, he said they'll become a focus. What's that got to do with you?"

"Am I Scottish? Am I German? Am I English, God forbid?"

As he posed those questions, he stood in front of the seated Humph. He bent forward, hands on his knees, staring hard at his friend.

"Stop this nonsense, Duffy. You're a one-of-a-kind wastrel. You're an unapologetic Irishman, for heaven's sake. God help us."

Duffy stood up straight, beaming.

"Damn right. I'm Irish."

"So?" said Humph.

"So, you ask. We Irish own the docks in New York. The FBI could never get a word out of us. And our old employers don't stand much of a chance either. By my reckoning, that leaves you and I, the future saviors of New York."

Duffy's statement made Humph realize he didn't want to get drunk or even close to being so.

He excused himself.

"Gotta go, my friend, but thank you. You've opened a door."

Back on the street, he felt excited. At the first pay phone he found, he called Higgins. He explained that crazy Duffy had hit the nail on the head as far as investigating possible Nazi influence surrounding New York docks.

"Only an Irishman can open tongues down there."

Higgins cursed himself for not having thought of that.

"I hate to admit it, but that damned Irishman is right. Come and see me in a day or two. We'll figure something out."

Humph felt rejuvenated. He felt useful again. He went straight home and lay down. He dozed off on the sofa, awakening only when Rebecca returned around 7:30.

"Good news," he said softly, extending his arms to welcome her.

"You rejected me. The Army rejected me. But Higgins and Duffy welcomed me with open arms. I won't be enlisting, ever."

Rebecca's glare melted. She sat on his lap and wrapped her arms around him. She didn't kiss him, but she buried her head against him.

Humph held on tight.

Over breakfast, he explained what Higgins had said to him, and tried to explain the importance of the Irish domination of the docks.

"Nothing is firm yet," he said, "but Higgins is working on a special anti-Nazi force to keep our docks secure. I'll be part of that."

"So, my stubborn hero, you're not useless after all." Rebecca laughed.

Humph kissed her.

"Where are my eggs?"

Playfully, Rebecca slapped his face.

Over breakfast, the subject turned to rationing. Fortunately, they didn't have a car, but they'd read that gas was being rationed severely. There was more to come, the newspapers said. Anything with rubber was about to be rationed, from automobile tires to golf balls, of all things. The Japanese now owned or controlled virtually all sources of rubber in the world. Sugar and meat would soon be rationed as well.

"We're entering a new world, Rebecca."

Rebecca said she'd overheard talk at the theater as well.

"We might be mounting special shows for guys undergoing training in camps around the country. And we'll probably be doing publicity for things like war bonds. Where we'll find the time, God knows."

CHAPTER 14

GUNSHOTS rang out at the east end of Fulton Street two days later. At first, the cops thought it was a truck-hijacking gone bad. The truck was heading west, away from the docks, and it was accompanied by a roar of bleating car and truck horns, suggesting a reckless getaway attempt.

However, all three men in the truck had been shot dead. The truck had rolled to a stop against the side of a delivery truck.

In the back of the truck, there was nothing of interest except that it didn't smell at all like seafood. There was nothing that was likely to have been stolen.

By the end of the day, two of the dead men had been identified. One was a well-known small-time criminal who actually still lived on the Lower East Side.

"If he'd had any sense ten years ago, he'd have moved out," said the investigating detective.

The second victim was identified by a bystander. He had no police record.

"That guy, he used to just hang around hoping for work of some kind," said a fish market clerk.

It appeared to be a matter for the traffic cops. The detectives bailed.

By late afternoon, they were back. A patrolman found a cardboard box with hundreds of leaflets urging dockworkers to stand united with anti-socialists everywhere. "Protect our docks from the Jews," read one line. It was punctuated with four exclamation marks. The patrolman asked one of the newly arrived detectives if this was Nazi stuff.

"Sure looks like it," the detective said, "and it ain't legal no more. The government shut down that Yankee-kraut Bund a few months back.

"Good work, officer."

Within the hour, police found similar flyers all over the docks, some just tossed aside and others stacked for handing out later, perhaps at a meeting of some kind.

"So," said one detective, "what made the guys in the truck take off like a bat out of hell? Who would be chasing them and shooting at them?"

That evening and the next day, the cops talked to merchants and dockworkers. No one had a clue what was behind the incident.

It was Duffy who recounted the case to Humph the next evening at the police pub. One of the officers seated near them overheard. He shoved his chair close to their table and confirmed the key elements of Duffy's description.

The three men were puzzled. By the end of the evening, when the subject had changed a score of times, Humph returned from the can and sat down heavily. At first, words didn't come out, but Duffy and the officer were transfixed by Humph's distorted face. As Duffy was to recount later, his friend had a distorted, almost diabolical eureka face glued in place.

The copper at the table yelled to the barkeep for another round. "This one's urgent!"

When it arrived, Duffy shoved a glass toward Humph's hand. He reached toward Humph and was ready to wrap his friend's hand around the glass if Humph didn't grab it. But he did. Duffy was relieved when words then came out of his mouth.

"Gentlemen," said Humph, looking at both men in the eye, "I have one word to say to you. Lansky." Humph's free hand slammed the table.

Duffy and the cop looked even more puzzled.

"My God, Duffy," exclaimed Humph. "Don't you remember I told you about Higgins letting me in on a secret when we started investigating these Nazi sympathizers? He swore me to secrecy and said the government had informed him they were seeking help from an amazingly wide range of sources. It was then that Higgins dropped the name of one of the most famous cultural icons ever produced by the Lower East Side: none other than Meyer Lansky, the most influential gangster in America."

"What about him?" said Duffy.

"He's Jewish. He hates the Nazis. He was born in Poland before his parents brought him here. No one hates the Germans more than the Poles. I don't know, Duff, but part of me suspects that Lansky, or at least his boys, were responsible for busting thousands of heads at that huge pro-Nazi assembly at Madison Square Garden in '39. I'm thinking that the government has asked our favorite gangster to keep his eye on the docks to make sure spies and propaganda guys keep far away. Just a theory, but I'll bet my fedora on it."

Duffy corrected him.

"It's really Rebecca's fedora. For years you wore it under duress."

The other cop spoke up.

"So you think Lansky's goons spotted the truck and gave the occupants a farewell party?"

"Exactly," said Humph.

From the bar, Humph phoned the precinct and learned that Higgins had gone home long before.

Returning to the table, he said he'd see Higgins first thing in the morning to pass on their theory.

"Can I join you?" asked Duffy.

Humph nodded.

"After all, my friend, the Lansky idea is no longer a secret now that the Bund has been shut down and we're at war. Obviously, the government will be doing everything in its power to keep the enemy off our shores."

Thanks to a gangster, Humph told himself as he walked home, he was now part of the war effort. He was also glad he could find his way home blindfolded. Curfew was in effect. Streetlights were turned off and curtains were closed in almost every tenement building he passed. Some people still had to learn they had no choice but to comply.

The next morning, Duffy phoned to say he'd wait for him on a bench in the park across the street. It was a beautiful winter morning, one of those days when the sky seems bluer than ever. It would have been nice to stroll through the park, sitting whenever there was an interesting point to make—about the investigation, about life, about war and peace.

Instead, they headed for the precinct. Humph didn't even buy the morning papers. They could wait.

Higgins was all ready for them. An officer brought three coffees to his desk as they arrived.

Normally, Humph was painstaking and methodical when describing a case under investigation, but this morning he couldn't wait to tell Higgins that what seemed like just another senseless New York shooting was in all likelihood an attempt by Nazi spies and instigators to bring the docks under their sway. After describing the events Higgins would eventually see in case reports from the detectives at the scene, Humph was ready to inform Higgins about the cherry on top of the investigation:

"Who shot these guys and why? How was that connected to the anti-socialist, antisemitic pamphlets found all over the place? I have you to thank for this, Higgins. Remember when you shared what was then top-secret information, namely that our government was willing to enlist gangsters to fight spies? Well, the only possible conclusion to yesterday's events was that these Nazi sympathizers had been sent packin' by Jewish patriots, namely Lansky or his boys."

"Bravo! Bravo!" Higgins said, almost shouting. "Humph, you've outdone yourself."

Humph beamed, which he did rarely.

"Except for one little thing," Higgins said.

Humph's face fell.

"Don't feel bad. You were so close to being dead-on right. The truth of the matter is this. While it is true that Lansky has been a big help in recent months, the most influential gangster when it comes to the docks is Charles 'Lucky' Luciano. As I'm sure you guys know, Luciano has huge influence over the waterfront and dockworker unions. Our government sees his cooperation as a way to prevent sabotage. We made a deal whereby Luciano provides us with intelligence about the docks in exchange for a commutation of his prison sentence."

"My God," said Humph.

"Your theory was brilliant, my friend, but you put all your money on the wrong gangster."

Humph chuckled at Higgins's summation.

"The good thing, the fascinating thing in all this," said Higgins, "is that we now have the two more powerful gangsters in the Mafia, Lansky and Luciano, working for Uncle Sam."

Duffy had a huge grin.

"Only in America, boys. Only in America."

CHAPTER 15

"I feel a chill every evening when the lights go out. Really, Humph. I have to start my breathing again. The Great White Way is now pitch black."

His walk home from the bar late the previous night made it easy to understand what Rebecca was describing, although he could easily imagine that the blackout would appear far more unsettling if you were around Seventh Avenue in the forties. Times Square in darkness? No one had ever seen that. No visible theater marquees. No bright lights shining on bejeweled celebrities entering lobbies in glittery gowns. Unimaginable.

"I try to imagine that belief in the world is restored inside the theaters, especially when the curtain goes up and the stage comes to life." Rebecca was a strong spirit, but she was also an artist who needed to express what effects life had on her.

Over supper, they kept one more light on than usual. At first, the gesture was done as a bit of a joke. But by the time dessert came, it felt good. It was like doing what you could to fight depression on a rainy day. As long as you were fighting, all was basically well.

"At least we're not hearing bombs descending on the city," said Humph. "I can't imagine what our allies in Europe are undergoing. You know, thousands in cities like London no longer have homes to go to. And those that do have homes, they don't know whether they'll be rubble the next morning. They sleep in subway tunnels so jammed their bodies are touched on all sides by the bodies of strangers. I read that the stench is unbearable."

"I'm not sure," said Rebecca, "whether that's comforting or the stuff of nightmares."

Later that evening, once the dishes had been done, they cuddled on the sofa and listened to the news on the radio.

Rebecca surprised Humph during a radio commercial break.

"I'm starting to agree with you that we should have joined the war at the beginning. Maybe not so many people would be in hell right now."

Humph's love for her at that moment was so strong he didn't know how to express it. Then she turned toward him and wiped away a tear that had started to travel down his cheek. He then knew he didn't have to say a word.

CHAPTER 16

FOR the next week, the world ignored Humph.

Rebecca was suddenly immersed eighteen hours a day in a Broadway show that was underperforming financially. The owners demanded an overhaul, and one in the shortest time possible because they didn't want to throw away the recognition their ads had already achieved. Shows had survived such refits, but the odds were definitely against success.

Eve had contacted him only once, to say that she had taken Christa on, with the permission of her mother, like her own daughter. In fact, Christa's mother moved in with Eve in case her daughter needed her. Eve's apartment, on 23rd Street, near Seventh Avenue, was small but somehow cozy. Burlesque and Broadway posters covered the walls. Cushions covered sofas and floors. It was not a family home, but it at least felt like Eve's home. Christa's mom loved it. She told Eve after moving in that it made her feel young again and independent, not a servant of an arrogant German. As for Christa, she had started talking openly to her mother. Eve made sure to be close at hand to make sure nothing accusatory was said by Christa's mom. She needn't have worried, however. The liberation her mom felt made her partner up with her daughter. They had a common enemy now, her husband, her dad.

Perhaps most importantly, Higgins was unreachable.

Humph felt like a single man again, a beginning detective with no contacts, a man with nothing to do but read the papers in the hope of finding a possible case to work on.

Strangely, the stories that would have interested him as possible cases had little appeal. Most of all, he wanted to read about the war. It was depressing: the apparently hopeless defense of Stalingrad against the Nazis, the unrelenting advances of the Japanese in the Philippines, the East Indies, Malaysia and Burma. Where next? As much of a reader as he was, Humph knew next to nothing of these places, but he could see that as inconsequential internationally that each place may have been, they were, stepping stones for the enemy.

When he expressed this one night to Rebecca, she astutely asked whether he was seeing himself as a boy hero flying over to those countries and bombing every enemy plane, singlehandedly vanquishing the Japanese and preparing to fly solo to Russia to demolish the German siege.

Half an hour later, he turned to face her in bed and said, "Yes. You're probably right."

Out of the war, feeling impotent, there was only one thing to do: become an ordinary citizen, doing his part. No more hero complex.

When he heard the NYPD was going to erect a stage downtown to sell war bonds, the humbled Humph asked if he could take part. He was welcomed with open arms by men wearing the same uniform he wore for years.

It was a cold, damp morning when he was called up to stand at the foot of the stairs to the stage festooned with Uncle Sam banners and American flags. To his surprise, though, hundreds and hundreds of people crowded around seeking to purchase the bonds.

Humph realized the war was being fought at many levels, not just crime fighting and military attacks.

He took part in the drive for two weeks, throughout Manhattan and the Bronx. He begged off just before the Queens portion.

He'd received a letter from a man he'd put in jail for art theft years ago. His name was Victor Garcia, a painter from Venezuela who had settled in New York, penniless. Somehow he got hired by an international art-theft gang and set up as an art restorer at the most prestigious art gallery in New York, the Met, the Metropolitan Museum of Art.

The message Humph received said simply:

"I know something about Nazi fundraising. If you would like to talk, I will tell you everything if we could spend at least ten minutes outside of this horrible prison."

Rebecca, too, had been part of a Broadway pitch to sell bonds. Their outdoor stage was different from the police department's. Broadway stars took turns singing popular upbeat songs.

However, when she and Humph met over supper that night, her crime-fighting antennae were on full-alert, just like Humph's.

Humph showed her Victor Garcia's letter.

Probably the only reason Garcia had confessed everything when he was first arrested was Rebecca's presence along with Humph, not because she was beautiful to look at and, unlike Humph, non-threatening, but most importantly, because he could plead his case in his native Spanish.

After talking at length with Rebecca about what Garcia could possibly have to deal with, Humph wrote a brief letter to be delivered to Garcia in prison, telling him there were a number of things they had to look into before such a visit.

The first step he and Rebecca agreed on was that only someone like Higgins could advise them on the legalities involved in such a negotiation with two people who were not employees of the NYPD. What could they offer Garcia? And what did Higgins think Garcia could offer them?

The next morning, Higgins's advice was for them to see Garcia on their own but in an unofficial capacity.

"Make it a fact-finding mission," the detective advised, "then report back to me, and if it looks like Garcia has useful information, I'll get the right people involved." Higgins wrote a letter of introduction on their behalf to give to the prison warden.

It was only when they got home that Humph looked at the original letter from Garcia. He was being kept in a prison about an hour's drive from the city, a dreadful place Humph knew only by reputation. It was called Sing Sing. It was famous for its Death House, where hundreds of the state's murderers met their end. It was the only prison in New York that carried out executions. Beyond that, all Humph knew about it was what he remembered from a James Cagney film a few years previous. The title escaped him. Although Rebecca hadn't seen it, she remembered the title: *Angels With Dirty Faces*. At the time, she thought that would make a good title for a Broadway show.

Since neither of them had a car, Duffy agreed to drive them. The car didn't belong to him either, but by some convoluted arrangement that Humph didn't want to question, the Irishman had access to it whenever he wanted.

"You understand, Duff, that I can't invite you in to talk to the prisoner."

"No problem, my love birds. As ugly as the prison's history is, it's located along the glorious Hudson River.

A good place for an old detective and his thoughts."

Humph made the coffee early the next morning. With a smile, Rebecca asked if she could hazard a guess that the person who made the coffee was not Puerto Rican.

Duffy signaled his arrival at Tompkins Square by honking.

Their chauffeur regaled them with stories from Sing Sing's past, which dated back to the 1830s.

"The unlucky bastards inside its walls were not allowed to say a word to anybody all day long, year after year. And when they were paraded to their worksites and to and from their cells, despite being chained, they had to put a hand on the shoulder of the lad in front of them. Everywhere they went, it was in lockstep. That, on top of the news of all those executions, must have rendered most of them stark ravin' bonkers in no time at all."

No wonder, thought Humph, Garcia referred to Sing Sing as a "horrible place".

As they drove, conversation lapsed. Duffy decided to revive it with a fact about Sing Sing.

"Did ya know that the joint has its own executioner? It's a full-time job. I wonder how he sleeps at night."

Rebecca couldn't help but think of her first meeting with Garcia, at the painter's co-op. Others identified him as the thin guy with the paint-stained T-shirt.

"How in God's name," she wondered, "could he survive even a day of physical labor?"

The sun was shining, and Duffy began to sing, quietly at first. From the back seat, Humph watched his friend closely to make sure he wasn't surreptitiously reaching for a flask of whiskey now and then. He wasn't. He then wondered what Duffy would be getting up to while he and Rebecca were inside the prison walls.

Once at the prison gates, a guard approached the car and addressed Humph. He presented the letter from Higgins to the warden. The guard held the car door open while

Humph and Rebecca exited. Later that night, Humph and Rebecca described the walk to the prison gates, then across a courtyard with guns pointing down at them from above. Their ears were not accustomed to the suffocatingly loud clank of the entrance gate. The guard led them to an upstairs office, marked "Warden".

The guard knocked, then entered the office. He returned seconds later.

"The warden has not arrived yet."

Standing in a prison hallway, with no benches or chairs to sit on, was as awkward as showing up unexpectedly at a universally hated aunt's funeral. There was nothing to do, nothing to say and no escape.

A podgy, well-dressed man arrived. He walked quickly, the heels of his well-shined black street shoes creating a pronounced but delicate, considering the surroundings, tattoo.

The warden shook their hands with a strange urgency and withdrew it seconds later as he entered his office, leaving them to follow uninvited.

The guard, who trailed them in, reached across the warden's uncluttered desk and presented the letter of introduction from Detective Higgins, NYPD.

The warden read it quickly.

"What possible interest could you have in a nobody like Garcia? I've never believed he had the mental equipment to be an international art smuggler. And here, at my prison, he's pathetic. He's barely able to pick up a sledgehammer. Nobody talks to him. The only thing to be said for him is that he causes no trouble. He's always as silent as a mouse. We like prisoners like that."

Rebecca was furious at the warden's thoughtless dismissal of a human being, especially one with the gift of art in his soul. Humph squeezed her hand hard enough to break through her thoughts.

"Sir," said Humph in his most commanding voice, "we

are here at the request of the prisoner, a person my wife and I turned over to the police originally. The prisoner, this Garcia fellow, says he has information that we would value greatly. We are not in the habit of ignoring possible leads of this import."

Rebecca was impressed. Humph hadn't exploded, as she would have, but the warden no longer leaned forward across his desk when talking. He had retreated. He was waiting for Humph's next words.

"We suspect that we are dealing with a case of international conspiracy to the benefit of America's enemy, Nazi Germany. In addition, we feel there is a possibility that your prisoner may knowingly, or accidentally, be aware of individuals devoted to the downfall of the world's greatest democracy. So if you can forget his physical ineptitude with a sledgehammer, the NYPD and the State Department would welcome your cooperation."

The mention of the State Department sealed the deal. Fifteen minutes later, Rebecca and Humph were shown to a windowless room with a table and three chairs. Ten minutes later, two hefty guards, holding Garcia's shoulders, deposited him heavily into the remaining chair. Humph stared at them until they left the room.

The instant the door banged shut, Garcia erupted in an explosion of Spanish directed solely at Rebecca. Humph could see that her eyes had become moist. It was not allowed, but he could see her fighting the urge to throw her hands around the poor man. Though it was Rebecca who broke the case against Garcia, she felt strongly that he confessed out of a love for art and that he had taken part in the scheme for the same reason. She still saw him as an artist, a poor one, far from home, not as an international criminal. Humph wondered whether that represented the difference between men and women, or whether his wife was simply right in not judging the Venezuelan harshly. Was it because she was an artist, too, someone who saw the world much like Garcia did?

After a little bit of small talk, Garcia began trying to explain what he'd learned from another inmate, and what theories he'd put together in his own mind.

He talked, in Spanish mostly, for some time. Humph had to remind him that the interview would be cut off shortly by prison officials.

"Be concise!"

In essence, Garcia had learned that Argentina had close ties with the Nazis and that, to support the Nazi cause, pro-Nazi businessmen and gallery owners in New York were arranging to steal valuable art in New York and send it to Argentina with the goal of indirectly helping the Nazis.

"We already know," he added, "that wherever the Nazis invade, they steal art of any value."

Rebecca stopped him.

"How would you hear of such things stuck in this hell? I'm sure they don't deliver the morning papers with your vomit-inducing breakfast."

Humph couldn't believe how articulate Rebecca had become in English. He felt his efforts to learn Spanish were pathetic in comparison.

Garcia had immediately raised his hand to stop her.

"There's a man here. His name is Arturo Valasquez. He is Argentinian. I can't remember what charge he was convicted of. It was minor. We're not friends. He's much older than I am. But one day we hid behind a wall being erected to enlarge the cafeteria and we talked. He told me most of Argentina wanted to be friends with Germany. They sold Argentina modern, technological things and bought their agricultural products. They also sold them weapons to prevent attack from Brazil, which hates the Nazis and is friends with the U.S. and British. They even sold them arms to keep out the U.S."

"So?" asked Humph.

"Delivering invaluable art to the Nazis makes Argentina important to them."

In the couple of minutes that remained for the interview, Humph and Rebecca pressed Garcia for facts about an art-theft and espionage network between New York and Argentina, facts they could present to the NYPD and the State Department.

As they rose to leave, Rebecca gave a little kiss to Garcia's right cheek. A guard loudly banged the bars to separate them.

"No contact!" he shouted.

Once outside prison grounds, Humph and Rebecca headed to Duffy's car.

They found no one inside, and the doors were locked.

They had no option but to search for him. They walked, hand in hand because it was such a beautiful day. They headed toward the Hudson River. At first, they spotted no one along the shore. Frustrated, they stopped at a burger stand. They ordered a burger and a soda, which they took to a riverside bench.

Before they had finished, a middle-aged woman with a bizarrely angular hair style came up behind them and inquired:

"By chance, are you looking for a distinguished Irish gent who says he's here on a mission of international importance?"

She led them to a knoll, not far from the river shore.

Duffy lay under a tree. He was on his back, his head was elevated against the tree, and in his hands, which crossed his chest, was a dandelion. On his face was the silliest smile imaginable.

How much he'd had to drink, Humph had no idea.

Humph had almost no experience, but he had learned how to drive. With no other option, engaging the services of the woman who led them to Duffy, they prodded him awake and all but carried him back to the prison entrance and the car.

All went well until they approached the city. Humph cursed almost every driver who passed him or offered him insulting hand gestures. After entering the Bronx, Humph pulled over. He was ready to explode. For a good half hour, they sat in the car. Suddenly, there was an explosion of obscene Irish mumbo jumbo from the back seat.

"Unhand this vehicle, sir!"

It was a revived Duffy.

Humph got out of the car and went to the back seat. He took his friend by the suit collar and hauled him outside.

"Stand up. Show me you can stand!"

To Humph's surprise, Duffy did just that.

Humph slapped the car keys into Duffy's hand and commanded, "Drive!"

Half an hour later, having held their breath all the way, Rebecca and Humph stepped out onto Avenue B.

CHAPTER 17

REBECCA couldn't take another day off, so it was Humph alone who went to see Higgins. To his surprise, when he got there, an officer from the U.S. State Department was there to greet him.

On Higgins's desk, coffee was already awaiting Humph's arrival. Humph had already fallen asleep the night before Rebecca, still outraged by Garcia's incarceration in such a place, had phoned Higgins. He wasn't in the office, but she demanded she be put in touch with him. When he replied, she provided all the details of the interview with Garcia.

The next morning, the State Department official said the government was absolutely interested in the plot "your friend" had unearthed. Although Garcia was Rebecca's "friend", Humph didn't object.

Over the following half hour, the State Department official gave him and Higgins a briefing to support why the government was 100 percent behind this lead.

He explained that since the very start of the war, Argentina had been walking a fine line.

"Argentina has technically remained neutral but has actively aided the Axis Powers. The country is teeming with Nazi agents, and Argentine military officers and spies are common in Germany, Italy and parts of occupied Europe.

"So," he added, "the possibility that your imprisoned painter has stumbled on something important is very, very likely."

Higgins asked how corrupt Argentina was.

The State Department officer pulled a file out of his briefcase.

"May I read something to you? It represents our current assessment of the country."

Higgins gave a wave of his hand. "Continue."

"Some Argentine politicians and military leaders have favorable views of Nazi Germany, which they saw as a counterbalance to British and American influence in the region. This sentiment is particularly strong among certain factions within the Argentine military and the political elite."

He concluded by saying the sale of stolen American art to Argentina made immense sense, either as a source of financing or to help out Hitler's latest dream. "He has plundered priceless art from every country he has invaded. We've heard that his incomparable ego has prompted him to declare that he is going to create a 'Führermuseum' in Linz, Austria to house all these works."

He added that because Argentina was still technically neutral, American citizens were free to send goods there, which was not the case with Germany. "It is strictly forbidden for us to ship anything to Germany. You could get in a pile of trouble for attempting to do so."

Humph, an ardent reader of newspapers, had to bite his tongue to keep his first thought from coming out. It had been disclosed that Standard Oil was shipping fuel to the Nazis via Switzerland. Just as bad, American-manufactured aircraft components were also making their way across the Atlantic, destination Germany. And where did the Nazis get so many Ford trucks? Such a comment made to the State Department official could make him change his mind about helping them with the investigation into the art thefts.

When Humph reported the State Department's enthusiasm to Rebecca, she immediately asked if that meant Garcia could be freed.

Humph had been so excited by the government's desire to take over the investigation he and Rebecca had created, he never thought for a second about Garcia's future.

The next day, Rebecca, after a long argument, got permission to skip work. She insisted Humph take her to the DA's office where she would argue that she, Humph and Garcia had negotiated an agreement that, if fulfilled, would warrant Garcia's freedom.

The DA hummed and hawed. "There's this to consider and that to consider."

"And bullshit to consider," said Rebecca. She said it in a calm voice. Humph loved her for that because it was so out of character.

The lawyer left the office to talk to an assistant.

When he returned, he said he was prepared to argue for Garcia's release in court.

Humph and Rebecca left flushed with victory.

When they reached the little park by City Hall, they sat next to each other, cuddling. Neither of them had expected the day to end that way. Maybe the system worked. The good were freed.

Humph waited, then said:

"No, the system doesn't know shit."

Rebecca stared at him from a foot away. "Where is that anger coming from?"

Several minutes later, the anger gone, Humph answered.

"Before you were born."

"OK. I like history. Lecture me, my dear."

Humph recounted his early days as a cop.

"While we used immigrants to build this city, they lived in squalor and were paid pennies for back-breaking work. Since they were supposedly living in the land of free speech, a lot of them complained out loud. It got them nowhere. They got lumped in with real anarchists at the time and, along with the bad guys, got imprisoned and deported."

Humph paused to order his thoughts. He didn't want to appear to be raving. That wasn't his style. Finally, he went on:

"The justice system and the holier-than-thou whites who ran things in the city used every chance they got to tell the world these people with unpronounceable names hadn't earned the right to be Americans and therefore couldn't enjoy the same rights. So many of these unfortunates lived in my neighborhood, Rebecca. Even though I was a copper, I lost all belief that justice was blind."

Rebecca moved close and hugged him.

The next day, Humph went to see Higgins. He suggested it would be useful if the painter were placed in his custody, his and Rebecca's, there in New York to facilitate questioning. Higgins said it would be a huge stretch to request that. Then Humph told him about Rebecca's talk with the assistant DA and his promise to look into granting the painter freedom.

"If we can add the fact that Garcia's freedom would greatly facilitate an ongoing, joint NYPD-State Department investigation, I think the case would become winnable. What say, Higgins?"

Higgins nodded.

"I'll call them."

Then he looked at Humph.

"Are you sure you're not just doing this to stay on Rebecca's good side?"

They both chuckled, then Higgins said, "Get out, my friend. I have work to do."

Humph hit the pavement again but this time in an optimistic mood. He was glad he had opened the door earlier so Rebecca could better understand the man she had married. And he was glad he got right to the point with Higgins on Rebecca's behalf. Then, as he walked up Broadway for no particular reason other than to feed his need to be moving, something happened that made him think the world was finally falling into place.

About an hour after leaving Higgins, Humph was walking slowly with his hands in his pockets. Suddenly, a shop door swung open, and a man barreled out of the store . . . right into Humph. He slammed into Humph's chest and dropped to the ground in front of the much bigger man. As Humph was reaching down to turn the man on his chest, a store clerk came through the door cautiously and said the downed man had robbed a bag full of jewels. The bag lay a few feet away from Humph. It had jarred loose from the thief's grip on impact.

The woman's husband had already called the police from the store. Humph held the thief down with his knee. When the officer arrived, he handcuffed the man. Humph didn't know him, but he readily agreed when the officer asked him to accompany them back to the police station. Once there, Humph asked the desk sergeant to call Higgins.

"Easiest arrest I've ever made," he told Higgins later. "Didn't even have to take my hands out of my pockets."

He couldn't wait to get home to tell Rebecca about his day.

That night, to celebrate the incredible day, Rebecca agreed instantly to Humph's request that they go to a jazz club instead of a salsa joint to celebrate.

"Jazz makes me think," he said. "Salsa just makes me feel good."

They went to a club called Smalls, on West 10ᵗʰ, just past Seventh Avenue. For the first time, Humph heard a bebop pianist, an extraordinary jazzman with a classical background. His name was Bud Powell. The music was so foreign to him that it gave him plenty to think about, if thinking was the right word for letting new sounds and rhythms pluck strings in your head.

On the way home, Rebecca admitted to being hypnotized as well, much to her surprise.

"I wonder what tomorrow will bring," Humph wondered aloud when they got home.

"Want to eat?" Rebecca asked.

Humph didn't answer. Rebecca finally found him already in bed, eyes closed. As Humph admitted the next morning when Rebecca demanded to know, "What happened to you last night? We were having a lovely, lovely evening, and then you disappeared!"

"Can't tell you how sorry I am, Rebecca. The whole day was incredible, and you were the best part of it. It was like, when we got home, I was in a dream and didn't want to wake up. That's why I ran to our bed."

Rebecca's mouth dropped open.

"Where the hell is the plodding, endearingly boring intellectual I married? Are you taking drugs? Are you going through a second childhood? Has the war driven you cuckoo or outright crazy? You've never been to war."

Finally, Humph replied.

"Rebecca, I don't know how to answer your questions because my mind has room for only one question right now. If New York art thieves are stealing paintings and sending them to Argentina, who pays the thieves? Argentina can't afford to do that. Besides, they only want the paintings because Hitler wants them. And he's not about to send a check to our local purloiners."

Not knowing who instigated the thefts, neither the cops nor Humph could advance the case. Humph stewed for the following three weeks until, miracle of miracles, Victor Garcia was released into the custody of the Barstals.

Higgins allowed him time to settle into a spare bedroom in Tompkins Square before summoning him, Humph and Rebecca to the precinct. When they arrived, washed, spit and polished, with Rebecca, who was always a sight to behold, Higgins led them to an interrogation room. There were no windows and there we no fans to keep the place bearable. However, comfortable chairs were provided in honor of the representative from the State Department and the attorney general for the Southern District of New York.

Because of the State Department's involvement, the case had shot to the top of the AG's agenda.

Humph whispered to Rebecca that she must remain silent unless spoken to. She pinched his thigh, hard.

For a moment, Humph forgot about the case. Instead, he wondered why Rebecca's response was a turn-on.

The AG was the first to speak.

"After reviewing all the evidence and the theories so far, from both Detective Higgins and the State Department, and the evidence provided by one of my assistant DAs derived from a Mr. Victor Garcia, since released from custody, it is clear that the thefts have been engineered by Nazi sympathizers in this city. They are in all likelihood American citizens, very likely of German heritage. Our sweep months ago of German-American spies did not include them because they went underground after the Bund was outlawed. They went about their daily business as would any American. They apparently did not seek out the company of known Nazi sympathizers."

It was the kind of long-winded statement only a lawyer could give, thought Humph.

"However," the AG continued, "our investigation into Nazi sympathizers was relentless. What we discovered was the existence of no fewer than five Americans of German origin operating art galleries in our city. We suppose that it is natural for art gallery owners to meet from time to time, but what captured our attention is that they frequently met in obscure bars or restaurants, far from their places of business and far from their homes. In fact, these places were rarely patronized by people of their standing. A low-life bar on the Lower East Side has to be considered as questionable."

He went on to explain that his office had investigated through Customs all shipments made in their names.

"Incredibly, if they are guilty of these art thefts, they made no attempt to disguise their identities when shipping the paintings to Argentina. I can only conclude that prior to the war, they had never been involved in illegal activity."

Higgins was the first to speak.

"That bodes well, sir."

"Indeed it does," answered the AG.

At that point, all eyes turned toward Victor Garcia. Rebecca looked under the table and saw his feet dancing out of nervousness.

"First of all," said Higgins, "tell me again who first told you of this theft ring?"

Rebecca spoke up. "Unless someone else present can do this, I would like to volunteer my services as a Spanish interpreter should the need arise."

The men looked at each other and finally nodded their assent.

"A prisoner who once served as a bodyguard for a British forger who worked here in New York for a couple of businessmen who were convicted last year for stealing art from the gallery where I worked, the Met."

Higgins stepped in and said, "The Wall Streeters involved have all been arrested and convicted. The only person not apprehended was the forger, who fled the country and, we believe, returned to England or Spain or Portugal."

The AG nodded toward Garcia again.

"He said a German kind of guy approached him a year ago, just before he was convicted, and said he would like to make use of the same system the forger used. He somehow knew about the Met case, where great artworks were brought in for repair, then smuggled out, leaving fakes done by the European forger in their place on the walls of the Met."

"How," asked the AG, "would he know about such a scheme?"

"The only way," answered Garcia, "was that he worked for them in some capacity, even a minor one like driving a getaway truck."

No further questions were posed for the proceeding fifteen minutes as the lawyers, government officials and detectives discussed the case among themselves in hush-hush tones. They had pushed their chairs away from the table.

Finally, the New York AG addressed Victor Garcia and said the country was grateful to him, and that after investigating his original sentencing, had decided that he deserved to be a free man.

Rebecca nudged Humph hard with her shoulder. Her smile was radiant.

The next step was to pursue the four or five Germans who had shipped goods out of the country to Argentina.

Higgins said:

"We have addresses. We have, as you know, interrogation rooms. Let's bring them all in."

CHAPTER 18

EVE knocked on their door unannounced. Her arm was around the young woman raped at the Andover Nazi camp.

Rebecca hugged them both hard and ushered them in.

Eve hadn't been in touch for weeks.

"I'm sorry about that," Eve said, "but things were going so well I didn't want anyone posing questions or putting things in doubt."

"Come, Christa. It's so wonderful to see you."

Unlike the last time they had met, Christa was able to smile.

Rebecca looked at Eve. Eve nodded. Christa was herself again. That's what Rebecca understood.

Rebecca offered to make lunch. Eve hugged a smiling Christa.

While eating, Eve asked if Humph had made any headway tracking down American Nazis.

"There must be scores of girls of German heritage who have gone through what Christa did."

Rebecca said she didn't know for sure, but she knew the case hadn't been dropped.

"Even the State Department is involved now," she said.

Eve gave a half smile but ended up looking suspicious.

Rebecca gave in and explained the art theft case involving Americans who supported the Nazis, the same guys who would have sent their kids to the Nazi camps. She said when they'd be arrested, some of them might give up information about cases like Christa's. "I can't be sure, Eve, but I sure hope so."

Eve and Rebecca then talked of other things for some time. "How is Humph?" "How is Broadway without lights?"

Finally, Eve announced she was going to adopt Christa.

"I want a family, but I don't want a man. My experience tells me that. They've all been bastards in the end."

Rebecca kind of knew what she meant. She knew she was lucky to have found Humph.

"What does Christa think of the idea?"

"I'm not really sure," said Eve.

"Despite our age difference, she thinks of me more as a sister than a mother."

Rebecca held Eve.

"In the end, does that matter? You can adopt her and still live like sisters, no? She'll soon be old enough to decide who she wants to live with."

Eve kissed Rebecca on the lips.

Eve slowly pulled away.

"Humph doesn't know what a jewel he has." After staring at Rebecca for a moment, she laughed like a little girl.

They returned to the living room. Rebecca sat between Eve and Christa and asked:

"How's work, Eve? Do you have a show again?" The question was her way of asking if she could afford to support Christa.

"No, Rebecca, but a producer I know well told me he's bringing a new one to Broadway next fall."

"Hell," said Rebecca, "knowing a producer means an all-but-guaranteed role. I'm thrilled. You deserve it!"

Eve, holding Christa's hand with her right hand, grabbed Rebecca's neck with her left, hauling her face against hers.

"Love you, Rebecca."

Eve and Christa left the apartment. There was no need for anyone to say a word.

CHAPTER 19

BUT Humph had a word or two to say when Rebecca recounted the news.

"Bless her." He was referring to Eve.

Rebecca got a call from her Broadway department head. It was the third of the day, yet it was only 10:30 in the morning.

"No choice, Humph. My master bids me to get my malingering ass to the studio in record time."

After Rebecca left, Humph decided to defy his usual habit when he had no specific task in hand. He firmly believed he could think only when walking aimlessly on crowded city streets. That day, he turned on the record player. He rifled through their record collection. Strangely, he took out two albums, both swing music, ones that he and Rebecca had often danced to when one or both of them had had successful days. It wasn't long before that on one of those soft, intimate dance nights, Rebecca had told him she really liked her life. He felt the same for himself but didn't say so out loud.

As late afternoon turned to early evening, Humph wondered how the police could make a case against the German-Americans for sending art to Argentina. In itself, that wasn't illegal. However, if, with the help of the young Venezuelan artist, Victor Garcia, they could assemble a case of a concerted effort by a gang of art dealers to steal from New York galleries in the name of Hitler, they might stand a chance. However, it would be hard to prove that an established New York art dealer was stealing the artworks everyone thought he was trying to sell. And how could they prove these dealers were acting in concert?

The Scotch Humph had been drinking while tapping his toe to the music suddenly shut off further speculation. He returned the albums to their sleeves and called it a night.

His sleep was short. Rebecca returned from work just after nine. Before she kicked off her shoes, the phone rang. It was Higgins, wanting to talk to Humph.

"He's sleeping so . . ."

"At this hour?" questioned Higgins.

"Yes," Rebecca answered, laughing. "Judging by the records on the coffee table, I'd say Humph has been dancing by himself and drinking Scotch all evening."

Higgins said he could barely imagine that scene. "Have him call me back when you get him upright."

Humph started the next day full of optimism.

"Rebecca, you and I are going to celebrate tonight."

When Humph arrived at the precinct, the mood was quite different—anything but triumphant. Two of the five supposed Nazi supporters in the art-theft ring had been assassinated.

Higgins was beside himself.

"Who could possibly notice who we had just arrested? It was just yesterday, for heaven's sake. And worse, who could have assassinated two of them?"

Humph pulled him aside.

"These Nazis, American Nazis, are everywhere. Hidden as ideal Americans. They're in our churches every Sunday. Their faith is sincere. Their congregations praise America and at the same time condemn anti-Nazi-Americans. The Christian church has proven itself time after time as a voice for oppression."

Humph led Higgins to a bench.

"Sit, my friend. We'll talk in a few minutes."

After letting Higgins cool down, Humph looked him in the eye and said the American Nazi base was much larger than he or the State Department had imagined.

Higgins had no response—at least not until the next day.

A German U-boat was spotted off a Coney Island beach. Two hours later, the Coast Guard reported that a merchant vessel, supposedly headed to England, had been stopped by the U.S. Coast Guard. When their report finally arrived at the police headquarters in New York, the truth was already evident. The boat was foreign, probably German.

A few hours later, the Coast Guard reported that apparent German agents had confessed that their mission had been to eliminate U.S. or British infiltration of their North American activities.

Neither Humph nor the chief of station for the Coast Guard could believe for a moment that the Germans would surrender that kind of information.

Late that evening, Victor appeared unannounced at Humph's place.

"Can I talk to both you and Rebecca? I'm sorry for giving you no warning, but I don't have a phone and I couldn't find change for a phone call."

"Come in," said Rebecca, standing behind Humph. "Have you eaten today?"

Victor shook his head.

"No job now," he said in broken English.

Humph sat him down on the sofa while Rebecca hurried to the kitchen to make him a roast beef sandwich, using leftovers from the previous night. While both men spoke more than a modicum of each other's native language, both felt tongue-tied without Rebecca's presence. In his discomfort, Victor turned and shook Humph's hand again, nodding and smiling. The awkwardness vanished as soon as she arrived with a towering sandwich.

They gave Victor time to dig in.

With the sandwich half consumed, Victor said in Spanish, then in English that, while he knew very little about the war and international relations, he had gained knowledge of the art world since coming to America.

"There was even a gringo art thief in jail with me!" He laughed at what he obviously felt was his good fortune.

"Sorry," Victor said upon seeing that neither Humph nor Rebecca seemed to understand his point, nor his little joke, if that's what it was.

"What I wanted to say to you was the more I learn about the Nazis stealing all the art they can find in Europe, the more I wonder why a Nazi lover here in America would send stolen art to Argentina. How would these American Nazi lovers profit from smuggling art out of the country? And what I find even more mystifying is how the Nazis would profit. Is there a reward for them in some kind of post-war Nazi heaven?"

Humph and Rebecca stared at each other. They could only shrug in response.

No one, be it the police or the State Department, had posed that question, yet now that Victor had put it on the table, it seemed like the most important aspect of the case. What was the motive of the handful of art smugglers?

The next day, Humph phoned Higgins to pass on the painter's question. The detective agreed completely that the answer to that question could go a long way in solving the case.

"We can't do much about that, however, until we catch one or all of the guys who have been sending art to Argentina. I'll get back to you as soon as I have news, Humph."

CHAPTER 20

IT was three long weeks before Higgins got in touch. He said he had "somewhat good" news. With the help of the post office and Customs, two men had been identified and apprehended on suspicion of theft and smuggling art. Both had used the same address in Buenos Aires.

However, both men, while admitting their Nazi sympathies, denied intending for the stolen artwork to end up in Germany. In separate interviews, they both asked, "To what purpose? What Nazi would pay us for art when they can loot what they want all over Europe?" All they could cop to, said Higgins, was hoping to get good prices for the art in an art-loving country with no connection to the U.S. They said they were just trying to make sure nothing was traced back to them.

"Do we know exactly where they sent the art in Buenos Aires?" asked Humph.

"Yes and no," said Higgins. "Both men sent the paintings care of general delivery at the post office in a poor section of the city. The recipient's name was different in each case, and city police down there were unable to find an address for the recipients. Both deliveries were picked up by men using Argentinian passports for identification, but their names, actually their passports, were likely fake. The Argentinian cops said that if these thefts involved big money, it was not at all beyond the realm of possibility that a local gang was happy to pay for the passports."

Higgins add that U.S. Customs gave him two more names worth investigating. "Let's wait until we nab them so we can compare everyone's story. Maybe something will slip out."

Hating boredom, Humph walked to the precinct on Mott Street to chat up the desk sergeant, an old colleague.

"Any more incidents of violence by possible Nazi supporters?"

"I have to admit, Humph," said the sergeant, "that people are seeing Nazi sympathizers in their dreams these days. Most cases we investigate are groundless in the end. However, we got a call not too long ago about a beating in a bar on Delancey around Norfolk. I don't know who hit whom."

"Can I ride along, sarge? I'm bored."

"Give me a minute or two. If I can, I'll assign a cop you might know, just to make the ride more interesting."

Fifteen minutes later, Humph was happily ensconced on the passenger's side of a patrol car. His "partner", behind the wheel, motioned for Humph to activate the siren. Humph felt like a schoolboy playing hooky.

When they got to the bar, beat cops had already cordoned off the entrance. A peek inside confirmed the outward appearance of the joint: sleezy.

Inside, they found a middle-aged man in cuffs. He'd been plunked down on a bar stool.

"At least give me a friggin' drink," he complained. "I'm the damned victim here."

On the other side of the narrow room, two young men lay unconscious by an overturned table. One man's shirt was soaked with beer.

Humph's partner for the day took his time questioning the beat cops and then a couple of customers who clearly had no intention of letting a scuffle deflate the foam on their beers. When he returned to Humph, perched on a stool next to the "victim", he summarized what appeared to have happened.

"The young gents, the ones by the overturned table, for some reason thought the guy next to you was a Nazi-hater. As early as it is—what is it, 2:15 p.m.—he's been on a pub crawl. At one of the bars, he gave a tongue-lashing to a young Nazi supporter, and our boys here overheard it all. Apparently, they rushed home and ran back with baseball bats. Finding that our 'victim' here had departed, they went from bar to bar until they found him here. The boys entered and, without ordering a brew, started batting practice. One of us, the constable by the door, just happened to be outside. His billy club, expertly wielded, proved enough to disarm and KO both Nazi boys."

The handcuffed "victim" next to Humph exclaimed, "Damned right, officer. I told them. I'm innocent."

A moment later, the handcuffs had been removed and the "victim" demanded a beer "this instant!".

After the youths had been deposited in a paddy wagon, Humph asked his partner if he had an address for them. "I want to find out if their parents are secret Nazi supporters."

Humph declined the offer of a lift back to the station. It was a pleasant May day. A walk was in order. He needed thinking time to digest the fact that sugar had just been rationed as part of the war effort. Somehow that seemed more important than the fact that American auto manufacturers had been told to stop making cars. And if you had a car, good luck getting replacement tires. Rubber was needed by the armed forces.

It was a good walk, but Humph felt almost as if he were wearing blue again. He set his course for the police pub. He rarely regretted having left the NYPD. Since doing so, his life had become a hell of a lot more interesting, and profitable. Although he'd done little of late to live up to his reputation, he still enjoyed a certain renown in the city. He was definitely in the mood for cop talk.

By the time he arrived, it was almost evening. The place still offered tables because the day shift hadn't gotten off yet. He was relieved. Although he could walk forever, he didn't want to stand at the bar all evening. He did, however, go straight to the bar to order a double Scotch.

"Humph, you ancient reprobate, what brings ya here?"

He turned and saw Duffy's face just inches away.

"Is this your damned retirement home, Duff? Where do you sleep, on the bar?"

"Not a chance, Sir Humph. I'm still the master of the Bowery. I figure city tour guides will start pointing me out soon. What have you been up to?"

Humph took a deep swallow of his Scotch.

"Actually, I've been playing cop all afternoon. Even got to put on the siren."

"Lucky man," said a grinning Duffy.

"In a way, yes," Humph answered.

"It reminded me that all cases lead to potentially interesting places. No detail is too unimportant to follow up."

He explained that the bar on Delancey held the key to a group of pro-Nazis that the cops didn't know about, ones who liked beating in the heads of true Americans with baseball bats.

"A great game, baseball," said Duffy, who'd never been to a game in his life.

As the day-shift cops got off duty, the din grew. Before it became unbearable, Humph managed to tell his friend about Eve's great accomplishment with the girl who'd been raped and beaten by an American supporter of the Nazi movement.

"She's come out of her shell and is thrilled that Eve is going to adopt her." Duffy, who had always gotten along well with Eve, was genuinely happy, even half drunk.

"What about police work?" he asked.

Humph started to explain the whole business of getting the Venezuelan artist released from jail and his great lead about a case of New Yorkers smuggling stolen art to Argentina, but the volume in the bar made him eventually throw up his arms in resignation.

Duffy leaned across the table and shouted, "More Scotch?"

Humph clapped him on the back and nodded.

In his mind, he was still wearing NYPD blue when he left the bar and headed home.

A week later, Higgins called him in to the precinct.

"We nabbed two more art thieves who sent artwork to Argentina. I thought you might like to sit in on the interrogation because more and more of everything seems related to the art forgery case you solved a while back."

"Me and Rebecca."

Higgins laughed.

"You're absolutely right."

"Anyway, care to join me today?"

"There's nothing else I'd rather be doing. Just a thought, though. I can't help wondering whether it might possibly help if Victor Garcia witnessed the interrogation of these guys. What think?"

Higgins considered the idea for a moment.

"I wouldn't want him in the room, but he could watch through the two-way mirror."

"Good call," said Humph. "Can we delay today's interrogation until I talk to Victor?"

"No, I've called in the State Department already."

"I'm not sure he's home, but he has no money, so he couldn't go far. Can you assign a car to take me to his place right now? No guarantee, but if we find him, there's a chance he could really help us."

Higgins agreed.

"I have other matters to discuss with the government guy as well. But do it fast."

Garcia had found a room in a three-story tenement in the Village. It wasn't much more than a flop house. Humph hadn't wanted to insult the artist by asking how much he paid for it.

Humph was excited when he found Victor home. Humph hurried him down to the patrol car outside, which sped, siren insisting on right of passage, back to Mott Street. On the way, Humph tried to explain the kind of evidence the police were hoping to extract from the two alleged smugglers, as well as the fact that he would have to wait outside the interrogation room.

"Maybe," said Humph, "their words will trigger something."

Then he added: "No one will be able to see you." With that, Victor visibly relaxed.

When they arrived at the precinct, they had to wait outside Humph's office until he finished talking to a government official. When the door started to open, Humph's long arm pushed Victor behind him to shield him from view.

Higgins and the official disappeared inside the interrogation room. Humph motioned Victor to a small, attached room. He sat Victor down in front of what looked like a window. "Like I told you, it's a mirror. You can see them, but they can't see you."

"We don't have this in Venezuela," Victor said, sitting down in front of the mirror.

Humph knocked on the door of the interrogation room to signal to Detective Higgins that Victor was in place behind the mirror.

Humph rejoined Victor.

One of the two men being questioned said he was a gallery owner.

"Why would I steal art? It's my business to display and sell it. You guys are out of your minds."

When asked why he had sent a painting to a general delivery address in Buenos Aires, Argentina, he answered with all the indignance he could manage, "I sent it to a client, someone who had purchased the painting on a visit to New York and returned to his home country. What do I care about where he asked me to send it?"

The State Department official calmly asked:

"If this Argentinian purchased the painting, can you show us a receipt for the purchase? It's our understanding that the painting was worth almost $80,000. An extraordinary sum. I'm sure, like any businessman, you would have verified that payment with your client's bank."

The man demanded to see his lawyer rather than answer.

He was taken out of the room for the moment.

The second man was brought in. He was asked identical questions.

His responses were day-and-night different.

"I don't know what to tell you. I was talked into all this. I've never done anything like this before. I swear."

Higgins took over the interview.

"Your criminal record, if you have one, is being checked as we speak. In the meantime, step by step, tell us how you got involved, who dragged you into this and what exactly you did in the furtherance of his crime."

Humph had spoken as if he were a judge passing sentence.

The man was clearly trembling.

"Your cooperation may serve you well in the end," said Higgins.

Finally, he spoke.

"The whole idea was that by sending our art to Argentina, to some kind of famous collector who supported Nazi ideals, we would be able to double our profits. I'm not sure how, but papers would be forged, and our paintings would be dangled before new buyers at much higher prices. We'd get a share of the profits from the increased value of the sales, and in the meantime, we'd get compensated for the theft by insurance companies here."

After a long silence, he added:

"Everyone said it was foolproof. The other guys said they'd done this sort of thing before and came out richer men. Me, I was losing money at my gallery. I was on the verge of bankruptcy. I couldn't resist their offer. All I did was follow their instructions."

He agreed that he'd sent the painting from his gallery to a general delivery address in Buenos Aires, but he couldn't remember to whom it was addressed.

"I was so much in panic that I just did what I was told, and then I wiped the whole thing from my mind. I swear."

The interrogation continued for an hour. The first man was recalled. He remained stubborn and was finally placed under arrest. When the second man was called back, he was in tears. His life was falling apart before the police came calling. Now his life seemed all but over. He was asked to name or describe every individual he had encountered while enacting his crime.

The police and the State Department had what they wanted.

After the two men were returned to holding cells, Higgins went to the room where Humph and the painter were waiting. He was smiling broadly. "Indeed," he said, "a beautiful day in May."

"But not quite," Humph said apologetically.

"That last witness, the one who admitted his crime but pleaded ignorance of the entire scheme? Well, Victor," Humph said, turning to the painter, "Victor got a feeling while listening to him."

"A feeling?"

"Yes, sir," said Victor. "When I was approached by the Wall Street broker himself, and then his underlings, they always spoke of great and easy profits for me. They knew I had nothing, and they played on that, just the way they played on your second man. I don't know, but it all felt identical."

"But these men, the ones we've just interrogated, are not involved with the forgery gang you speak of," said Higgins, revealing more than a little frustration.

Humph was surprised when the little painter continued to speak up.

"They kept assuring me I'd have nothing to worry about, always adding that my future was assured. I started to believe them. They explained how minor my task would be. Just make the minor repairs to the paintings and keep my mouth shut."

"What," demanded Higgins, "is similar to our current case?"

"The reaction of that man. He's no criminal and never has been. But he sensed he needed to be afraid. That's exactly how I felt."

Victor paused. When no further questions were thrown at him, he said he started to understand that some higher power must be in charge of the whole operation.

"You've got to ask all these suspects about absolutely everyone they heard of as being involved. In my case, it was the famous international forger, from Britain, I think. I never saw him or spoke to him. I don't think many people ever did. But I'm sure now that it wasn't the broker who ran everything. It was the foreign forger."

CHAPTER 21

HUMPH took Victor home with him. He'd earned another hearty meal and more. He was so impressed with Victor's English at the police station, he decided to say so by trying to tell Rebecca in Spanish that the painter was amazing and of great help. He said, "*Victor fue* incredible *y un gran ayuda*." Rebecca gave him a quick kiss and a smile before correcting him. She said, "*Victor fue increíble*, not incredible, *y de gran ayuda*, not *un gran ayuda*." She kissed Humph again. This time it was a longer one. "You get a mark of 99 percent on your Spanish report card."

Victor applauded and demanded, "Encore, encore!"

An hour and a half later, over supper, Humph was emboldened, freely sprinkling his English in with Spanish. No one corrected him. Neither Rebecca nor Victor felt quite so far from their roots.

All went well until Victor, looking at Rebecca, said this was a day for celebration, for the advances they'd made in the art smuggling case, and now for Humph's Spanish breakthrough. "We should celebrate by teaching Humph how to dance to salsa."

"That would be a perfect way to end the day," Rebecca agreed. She had already tried to teach him, and, admittedly, her reluctant husband had made an effort. Still facing Victor, she said the key would be loosening him up beforehand. "You pour him a big Scotch, and I'll put on the music."

Humph tried to put off the inevitable by staying in the dining room and clearing the table. Just as he was about to brush the crumbs from the table, Rebecca snuck up behind him and pinned his arms as if she were a cop doing a takedown. She marched him to the living room.

Victor cranked up the volume, and Rebecca spun her captive husband around to face her. She took his left hand and, as if in an automatic reflex, his right arm embraced her. Her hips showed Humph the way. Victor was dancing by himself. There was a huge smile on his face. Suddenly, Rebecca dropped Humph's hand and grabbed Victor's. As she and her new dance partner spun around, she was delighted to see Humph smiling and gently gyrating to the music. Moments later, she pirouetted and landed back in Humph's arms.

CHAPTER 22

REBECCA had to work the next morning. Humph accompanied Victor to his room in the Village, then retraced his steps eastward as far as the Bowery. He arrived at Duffy's place around eleven. He figured the chances of his friend being awake and functioning at that hour were about fifty-fifty.

Duffy was still navigating the caffeine portion of his morning. Humph, mildly hungover, gladly accepted a cup.

Duffy was alert, and not long afterward, Humph felt the same. For some strange reason, Humph felt younger. Duffy seemed that way, too. It was almost as if they'd lost twenty years and were the eager beavers of crime-solving, the way they once were.

He told Duffy that.

The Irishman laughed.

"It was good to have energy, to be up for anything, my friend. I guess that's no longer the case."

After a long pause, he said, "I guess that's why I'm always, or almost always, happy to see you. You bring the hope of undertaking a young man's chore."

Before Humph could reply, Duffy added:

"You know that expression you used, eager beaver? Well, I'm told it comes from the Great War. It described a young recruit willing to do anything to defeat the enemy even though he had no bloody idea how indescribably murderess the real battles were."

Humph was much younger than Duffy, at least that's what he had always thought. Perhaps the age difference wasn't so great if Duffy's lifelong boozing and partying had finally taken its toll. Humph liked to drink. His immense frame could handle a lot of booze. But he had never been a partier.

"The case I'm working on, Duff, it's an interesting one."

It was also a complicated one. He spent almost an hour explaining the ins and outs, describing the Nazi-loving New Yorkers hoping to become rich by having some forger make it possible to sell their own art, or art they stole, to a rich Argentinian, Nazi-loving art collector.

"The forger, Duff, he's the key. He's the key because he makes the artwork legitimate by changing its history and ownership. When the rich Argentinian buys it for an inflated price, there is no trace of its legitimate history. The forger takes a big share of the inflated price, and our American traitors here in New York take theirs."

He explained that Higgins and the federal government had already apprehended the New Yorkers who sent paintings to Argentina.

"Nothing conclusive yet," Humph said, "but we're starting to figure out who we're really after. It's the forger friend of the rich Argentinian."

"A long, long way away," said Duff.

"Right you are, but if you remember my last big case, the theft from the Met—you know, the Metropolitan Museum of Art—you might remember that we caught everyone involved, the Wall Street biggies, the gallery owners, everyone but one person. That one person, we're learning, was the real organizer and boss of the operation. He fled to England before we could catch him, and we lost track of him there. He may not even have been English.

"Anyway, Duff, thanks to the guy we nailed in connection with all this, the guy who helped put invaluable pieces of art in the hands of the bad guys, we now think the new scam is being orchestrated by the same man, the supposedly English forger, the one we almost nabbed here."

He said no one knew for sure, and added that Higgins was still trying to digest all these circumstantial leads.

"But the case, in my opinion, is very much a New York case, an American case. We just can't prove it."

Duffy nodded slowly, letting the facts sink in. Then, in slow motion, he stood and headed to the shelf with the booze. He took a glass and turned to Humph with a questioning look on his face.

"No . . . yes," said Humph.

They drank in silence for a good ten minutes. Finally, Duffy broke the silence.

"Why don't you go to Buenos Aires and interrogate the collector?"

Humph had never thought of that.

"Maybe," said Duffy, "he might, under whatever duress you can bring to bear on a big shot down there, get him to cough up the name of the mastermind of this whole scam."

He went on after letting the idea sink in.

"Do you think the government there would help you or at least the local cops?"

Humph said he didn't know much about the country, but from what he'd heard from the U.S. State Department guy at the interrogations, the art collector was super wealthy and powerful. He liked the Nazis, and so did a huge proportion of government officials and politicians.

"They don't trust us or the Brits or Brazil, which has close relationships with all of us. That's why they say they're rooting for the Germans, for self-protection."

Duffy took a swallow and said:

"All the more reason to go there and stick your nose into the art world there."

Humph declined a refill. His mind was in overdrive. He needed to talk to Higgins and the government guy.

Before heading to the precinct, he decided to phone. He learned only that Higgins was gone for the day. All they could say was that he left with government officials earlier in the morning.

Although by no means drunk, Humph wanted to be as alert as possible. He went to a diner on Rivington, not far from Duffy's place. After settling in there, he realized Duffy's quick suggestion that someone had to visit the rich collector in Argentina was dead-on accurate. The New York smugglers couldn't possibly know the inside workings of the scheme. If his old case involving Victor at the Met meant anything, this operation was being conducted in the same way. The right hand didn't ever know what the left hand was doing. That meant guaranteed untouchability for the real propagators of these crimes.

Humph came within inches of banging his fist on the table in frustration. Law enforcement was being made a fool of.

When he cooled down, he realized the one friend he hadn't consulted in the case was Gerald Franklin at the New York World-Telegram. When Humph was still an NYPD beat cop, he had gotten to know Franklin. Compared to most reporters, Franklin seemed to respect the difficulties cops faced. In time, Humph learned he could trust him. Franklin was just a cub reporter in those days. Humph consulted him often and watched him rise to city editor to managing editor of one of the city's most-read papers.

Humph ordered a Danish to go.

When he got to the paper on Park Row, the Danish was long gone. On entering the building, he waved his press pass, awarded by the paper after collaboration on several of his big cases. Humph still didn't know how to type, a fundamental skill for reporters to possess, but he found the newspaper game exciting.

When he reached the newsroom, Humph was taken directly to Franklin's office.

"Bad day for jawing and reminiscing," his friend said the instant he saw him. "My boys have just gotten the goods on a city councilor for accepting a ton of bribes from contractors in the hunt for city contracts."

"Won't keep you long," Humph said, taking a seat in front of Franklin's paper-strewn desk. "What I mainly want to know is whether you guys have a correspondent in Buenos Aires. I want to find out what I can about this incredibly wealthy, high-society art collector who also loves Nazis."

Franklin had to think for a moment.

"Yes, now I remember. We have a guy who used to work for our State Department but after about ten years grew sick of bureaucracy. Long story short, he had been assigned to Argentina at one point, although I don't know why. He met a beautiful Argentinian woman, married her and quit his government job. He speaks Spanish, which is maybe one of the reasons why State sent him down there. All I can tell you is that our world desk started using him for the occasional story a few years back. I'll have to dig up his name and address for you. Can I give you that by phone? As I said, the joint's jumpin' right now."

Humph was delighted. He knew his desire to travel to the country would need solid investigative possibilities to get the approval of the NYPD and the government.

CHAPTER 23

THE next day, Gerald Franklin called Humph early. So far un-caffeinated, Humph listened as the newspaperman said the paper's correspondent in the land of tango, art, wine and gauchos would love to try to get close to the snooty collector. "He asked that you send him a letter describing what you're looking for about the guy."

Humph interrupted.

"You can just send him a telegram saying we suspect that the guy is up to his bolo tie in fine-tuning art thefts at the behest of a European forger who used to work in New York and could still be instigating thefts here. It's the forger we want, not the collector."

"Got it," said Franklin. "I'll keep you posted."

Not long after Humph had finished his first coffee, the phone rang again. It was Higgins.

Humph told him about arranging to get the Argentinian correspondent for the New York World-Telegram to try to get close to the collector in the hope he might let slip some information about the forger, their Mr. Benjamin Borasco, or whatever his current name was.

"Excellent," said Higgins. "I was actually calling to talk to you about another possible avenue for tracking Borasco down. The State Department is not going to send anyone to Buenos Aires, but with the start of the war, the president has recently set up a new agency. It's called the Office of Strategic Services, OSS for short. Its job is intelligence gathering and special ops in support of the war effort."

Higgins added:

"If we need help in tracking Borasco's activities, the OSS might be able to do that for us. Our New York art theft cases won't interest them much, but the fact that the collector is a Nazi sympathizer, added to the fact that our best guess at the moment is that Borasco is funneling forged art to the Nazis, well, that definitely would interest the OSS. Everything that helps the Nazis hurts the U.S. and our allies."

Suddenly, Humph realized that the good news about the OSS deflated an unexpressed personal wish. Far in the back of his mind was a fantasy about he and Rebecca being assigned by the NYPD or the State Department to head to Buenos Aires at some point to investigate what both the New York World-Telegram was doing and what the OSS might do.

Like the Cuba trip the year before, designed to follow a New York art thief, a case that Duffy miraculously solved, going to Argentina would thrill Rebecca, who would accompany Humph as his translator. Humph had even daydreamed, in those micro-second flashes that make people skip a line in the book they're reading, that such a trip, despite its seriousness, would be like yet another honeymoon.

"Are you still there, Humph?" Higgins asked.

"Yes, yes. I was just trying to think about what all our options might be." He would keep quiet about the idea of getting assigned to head to South America with Rebecca.

"In the meantime, Higgins, do you have any local cases I might look into?"

Just as Gerald Franklin had done earlier that morning, Higgins said:

"I'll get back to you on that, Humph."

He phoned Eve. No answer.

He phoned Rebecca at work. Someone else answered.

"I'll track her down and get her to call you back."

He was about to pour a stiff drink and stretch out on the sofa when Rebecca returned his call.

"Feel like some jazz tonight?"

"If we can dance to it," she replied. When he didn't reply immediately, Rebecca said she knew a place.

Humph couldn't say no. To himself, he thought, "Might do me some good."

Late in the afternoon, Higgins called back.

"Got something for you."

He said it was yet another Broadway-related case.

"A dancer was murdered at a casting call for a new show," Higgins said. "We've talked to the other dancers and the casting director. Nada. Thought maybe you and Rebecca, with your contacts, might help loosen a tongue or two."

Humph jumped at the opportunity. After Higgins gave him the particulars, he left a message for Rebecca. "No dancing tonight. Higgins gave me a case, about a murder during tryouts for a new Broadway show. Need your help with this one. Come home soon as you can."

When Rebecca arrived around five o'clock, much earlier than her usual hour, she announced before sitting down that she'd already made inquiries into the murder. "All of Broadway is talking about it. It's scary for everybody."

Humph poured her a drink.

"Supper can wait," he told her.

Within two or three sips of her drink, Rebecca had calmed down enough to coolly reveal what she had heard about the stabbing.

"The girl who did the stabbing and the victim had apparently been lovers until about seven months ago. They had lived together in a small apartment on the west side, down around Houston, for some time, apparently. I couldn't find anyone who could say what went wrong between them."

Humph asked what she'd heard about the incident itself.

"A dancer, in workout gear, couldn't easily conceal a weapon, could she?" he asked.

Rebecca said she didn't really know.

"Can you take some time off tomorrow morning to go to the scene with me?" Humph asked.

"Yeah. Sure. There's not a lot going on right now that needs me."

Humph hadn't heard that news for ages. Rebecca always had a million things to do, flitting from show to show. That was the downside to having earned a huge reputation for skill and imagination.

By the time Humph had rolled out of bed the next morning, Rebecca was already hitting the phone.

As Humph entered the kitchen to pour a coffee, Puerto Rican style, Rebecca called out:

"Got the address where the tryout was taking place, and got a number for the casting director. She'll be available around 10 or 10:30 this morning."

The show had tentatively been called *Stardust Makes Me Sneeze*. Apparently, it was a take on celebrity intoxication in both Hollywood and Broadway.

When Humph and Rebecca arrived at the rehearsal studio downtown, the casting director hadn't yet arrived.

However, most of the tryouts were already there and waiting for their go at the golden thumbs-up moment.

Humph and Rebecca moved in.

Rebecca introduced herself to the girls. The veterans of previous shows already knew her.

"We all know what happened yesterday. A tragedy, one that I can't imagine having witnessed. What we don't know is why. Talk to us. We need to know everything that might give us the why. Who among you knew the pair outside of work?"

Two girls raised their hands.

"May we talk to you for a moment in private?" Humph asked.

They both nodded.

Rebecca mentioned to Humph as they walked to an adjacent room to question the girls that they were auditioning for a show called *Yankee Doodle of the USA*. It was not scheduled to open until December, six months away.

Each girl said the two dancers were lovers. All of a sudden, they said, they appeared to be bitter enemies.

"I don't know for sure," said one of them, a statuesque brunette seemingly too tall to fit in a chorus line, "but I heard the girl that got stabbed had an affair with an actor from another show. I think he was in *All in Favor*, a comedy that opened at the start of the year."

The second girl said she'd heard the same rumor.

"Why would anyone throw away a Broadway career over jealousy?" she asked.

Rebecca said: "Good question, dear, but I sometimes think love messes us up more than it delivers us." Humph felt a chill. He had never really had a relationship before Rebecca.

When the casting director arrived, Humph and Rebecca surrounded him immediately.

He insisted on being allowed to tell the aspirants to warm up.

In the makeshift interview room, Humph took out his notepad and calmly asked for a moment-by-moment account of the stabbing.

The casting director said simply that the girls had taken their places for an ensemble trial.

"By that I mean, I wanted to see whether they could dance in tandem with other girls in the chorus line, do their steps accurately and in time, look happy, you know, all that minutia.

"At the first break, the girl who ended up being stabbed had sat down for a breather, as many of them do. I wasn't paying much attention, but I was staring at some of the girls who caught my eye. I didn't know their names, but I wanted to be able to pick them out for final selection. All of a sudden, the girl on the floor screamed and rolled over. Another girl had a knife raised to strike again. She was screaming something, but I couldn't make out the words. A stagehand tackled her. We held her until the cops arrived."

Humph told him he could go back to the rehearsal room.

Sounding more like a cop than ever, Rebecca said:

"A cut-and-dry case. Yes? No?"

"We should talk to the actor she had the affair with before we shut down the investigation. Broadway is indeed a beautiful world, but it is competitive beyond my imagination," said Humph. Rebecca couldn't argue otherwise.

It was two days before they were able to contact the actor the dead girl had had an affair with. He lived on the Upper West Side, in the 70s, in a building with a doorman. It was a long way for the tenement the girls had shared downtown.

Although he gave Rebecca a long look when they entered, he quickly became irritated at their "intrusion".

He protested that he had a show to prepare for that very night.

"I don't give a damn about that," said Humph stepping closer to him so that his huge frame might encourage the actor to become conversational as requested.

In the end, he admitted to the affair. "Just a fleeting thing."

"Do you realize that it got her killed?" interjected Rebecca. She was suddenly in her "god damn males" mood.

The actor said he didn't know anything about that.

"For some reason," said Humph, "I don't believe you."

The actor relaxed. While formidably basso, Humph's voice wasn't emotional like Rebecca's.

"It's a long story," the actor said, collapsing into an armchair.

"I heard about the stabbing. I knew the dead girl."

"You more than knew her," said Rebecca.

The actor sank further down in the big easy chair.

Humph put his hands on the arms of the chair and leaned over him.

"It looks like you knew she'd be murdered, a girl you'd slept with."

The actor squirmed, raising a hand to distance Humph, whose face was a foot from his. He couldn't budge Humph an inch.

"Stop wasting our time," said Rebecca.

"Yes, I knew she'd be killed. Are you satisfied?"

"Not in the slightest," said Humph.

The actor was silent.

Humph moved his face closer.

"OK. OK. The girl had learned that I slept with the producer of my show to get the role."

"So what?" said Rebecca.

"You have no idea what this business is like, girl. I could lose my role, or I could be blackmailed. God knows what."

Rebecca stared at him, suddenly as calm as can be.

"I think I know what this business is like. I've been in it almost since I was a kid."

The actor realized he was dead meat.

"Fuck!" he wailed. Covering his eyes with his hands, he wept.

Twenty minutes later, he admitted to telling the dead woman's girlfriend that he had slept with her, at her insistence. He told her he had no idea at the time that she had a girlfriend. All that mattered, he told the girl, was that she had betrayed her.

"And she could betray me. I can't explain right now, but she had to disappear, for her sake and mine."

Humph let Rebecca pull the handcuffs from his belt.

"He's all yours, dear."

Together, they marched him downstairs to the lobby. Humph pushed him down into a chair and used the concierge's phone to order a police unit to affect the arrest.

"Care to go dancing?" he asked Rebecca.

"I don't know, Humph. I'm too turned on to want to go dancing."

They grabbed a cab to Tompkins Square.

CHAPTER 24

"HELL, Humph, you just closed a case before we had time to enter it fully in our records."

Humph liked the praise, but when he laughingly responded to the praise, he said he had to admit that "Detective First-Class Rebecca Barstal deserves the credit."

Before ending the call, Higgins said he had met with a man from OSS.

"I told him about the case involving our forger and the rich collector in Argentina. I mentioned your work on shutting down the operation in New York. He asked for your phone number. He was interested in the fact that you knew how he operated in New York, and that you knew specifics about his methods from an artist who had been convicted at one point, one who'd been somehow connected to the forger."

Higgins added that the agent never said they'd be going to Argentina. He just wanted confirmation that this international forger had lived there in New York and was clearly involved in a forgery network being utilized by the Argentinian collector. He admitted they didn't have absolute proof, but the link between the two New York smugglers they had nailed and the collector in Buenos Aires made it seem very likely.

Higgins finished by saying thanks once again for that day's efforts. He then added:

"Haven't got anything else for you at the moment. You've earned a little vacation."

Humph did reply with a regard to the suggestion, because Higgins surely knew he was incapable of taking a vacation.

A few days later, a "vacation" included three calls to the New York World-Telegram's managing editor and friend, Gerald Franklin, and one to Duffy, his Bowery buddy; Humph was hot to trot. However, he didn't know exactly where he wanted go. He was hoping that an afternoon at a pub with Duffy might point him in the right direction.

Duffy said he had to decline the invitation for that day, but his schedule was clear for the following day. He explained that his self-appointed task for that day was to hunt down a lovely *amiga* who lived in the South Bronx off Third Avenue.

Humph didn't need to know more. He already knew that if Duffy found his Hispanic lady friend, the odds of him being sober the next morning were slight.

"On second thought, Duff, I'll see you in two days."

That evening, Rebecca didn't hesitate for a second in accepting his suggestion that they step out so he could practice his salsa skills.

On the way to a club in Harlem, Rebecca said:

"We won't need to practice much longer. For a huge guy, you're actually getting quite good."

Humph loved the compliment, but he gave all the credit to his dance partner, adding, "I can't remember her name at the moment." Her left elbow was surprisingly sharp as it attacked his ribs.

It turned out to be a late night, a fun one, but much later than they had intended. The next morning, few words were exchanged as Rebecca prepared for work and Humph searched for a handful of dollars in preparation for his Duffy day. Humph had the advantage because Duffy would offer some hair of the dog to restore him while Rebecca would have to go cold turkey at her job.

Mid-morning, Duffy was annoyingly chipper.

Duffy was quick to diagnose Humph's problem.

"I prescribe Irish whiskey, not Scotch," he pronounced with all the authority of a real doctor.

Humph didn't have the patience to argue.

As the booze slowly softened the edges of his universe, Humph announced to Dr. Duff that he was cured.

Duffy bowed.

"So, boyo, what's on your mind?"

Humph paused to collect his thoughts of the past few days.

"Duffy, you've read about the countless Americans who applauded Hitler's philosophy, if you can call it that. Now that we've taken up arms, they've grown a lot quieter. The last thing they want is to be imprisoned or deported for treason. However, I've been reading, Duffy."

"Good for you, Humph. They say reading broadens our mind."

"Can you not get serious for a moment?"

Duffy spread his hands in a welcoming gesture.

"It's one thing for a domineering husband and father in Andover or Hamstead or Astoria to say heil Hitler. It's another for an American corporation to make investments that benefit the Nazis, that give them the financing they need to build arms."

"No argument there."

"The State Department told me and Higgins that they've already investigated Lindberg, Henry Ford, the Chase bank, name it. Other people I've talked to say there are a lot of Wall Streeters intentionally or inadvertently helping that fucking Führer guy, even now, after he's sent submarines to our coast and U-boats to sink the arms and supplies that we're trying to send to England. Hell, sometimes you can spot a German sub from the beach on Coney Island."

"And?" said Duffy.

"And?! Hell, Duffy, the krauts are killing guys in our merchant marine; they're trying to tell us they can invade America whenever they want. They're sending our arms and supplies to the bottom at will. And what pisses me off to no end is that there are money guys in this city helping their cause, not out of belief in Nazi values, but for the good old American belief in profit at any price."

Duffy had not failed to notice that the big guy had stood up to add emphasis to his patriotic rant.

He let Humph sit and squirm for a good ten minutes.

"What's your plan?" he asked, knowing full well that Humph always had a strategy. He was too rational to be satisfied with an emotional outburst.

"I don't have a good plan. But I can't help but feel there are some Wall Streeters worthy of prison for treason. I need help in nailing them for whatever, even if originally it has nothing to do with Nazis."

"Hell, Humph, can you be any vaguer? Talk straight."

Humph nodded, then held up his glass for a refill.

"Over the past couple of months, I've been keeping half an eye on a Wall Street banker, a young guy who likes to play Mr. Irresistible in upscale clubs. Dresses flashy. Cocky as hell."

Humph said he knew as a fact that the guy has arranged investments in major German corporations, big-time ones like Krupp.

"They're huge suppliers of armaments to Hitler. We already know they are starting to use slave labor in their factories. So how could an American invest in them? That would be treasonous now."

"I gather your cocky banker is doing just that. So, tell me, Humph, how do you want to bring him down?"

Humph explained that several of his contacts had told him the millionaire Wall Street banker liked dressing as a woman, a German woman. His favorite role-playing was performing as a German cabaret singer. "The guy has money to burn. The reason so many people know of his penchant is that he throws lots of parties, themed ones, you know, 'A Naughty Night in Berlin', that sort of thing."

Humph added that he'd even learned that the banker developed his character at a brothel in the Tenderloin District of Manhattan. There was one on 47th Street near Fifth Avenue that he favored. "If you have the dough, you could get anything you want."

Duffy laughed.

"I'll have to try it out."

Humph raised his glass. Duffy's unflinching degeneracy deserved a toast.

Humph resumed.

"I've been giving this a lot of thought. Maybe I'm a sadist at heart.

"I want to nail him at his most embarrassing moment, a moment that all his investors would find repulsive. I want to shut him down. If we can arrest him for something like lewd behavior or simply frequenting a brothel, we will have a chance to grill him about his Nazi sympathies and, most important, his investments. We'll have the right to look at his books."

"How do we go about doing that?" asked Duffy, obviously intrigued at the prospect.

"I'm going to talk to Higgins. If he can affect the arrest, all the better."

WAYNE CLARK | Humph's War

Duffy looked disappointed. He'd never been inside a brothel in Midtown that catered to a moneyed clientele.

The next day, Humph called Higgins and explained who he wanted to bring down and why.

"It must give you a backache, but I must say having your ear to the ground pays off, Humph."

After Humph chuckled, Higgins said simply:

"You determine when and where. Try to track him leaving his apartment dressed for a special occasion of some sort in the evening. Something like that. Follow him to his destination, which I hope will be a brothel. Call my night shift commander and ask a bunch of guys to arrest this fellow. I will have already filled him in. Call me the next day. I want you in on the interrogation."

Humph called Duffy.

"Ya think they'll invite me in for the interrogation?"

"No idea, Duff, but Higgins won't object if you watch."

"That calls for a celebration, Humph."

"Since I might end up participating in the interrogation, I have to stay sober. As for you, just be yourself, Duffy. If you're totally sober, no one will recognize you."

The weather turned foul over the next couple of weeks. Higgins and Humph took turns staking out the banker's place in an Uptown high-rise, doorman and all. In no time, Duffy befriended the doorman, who was as cold and bored as Duffy on blustery nights.

"Only in New York," the doorman explained one night. "I'm from Idaho. Never see anything like this back home." He'd seen the banker in full drag, makeup and all, even a long cigarette holder. "Off he goes in a limo. Usually returns just as the sun is rising."

The doorman said the banker only went out on Saturday nights. "He works really long hours during the week."

That information made the surveillance operation a lot less demanding. Wanting to be in on the kill, Duffy told Humph he'd be happy to take the watch every Saturday.

On the third Saturday night vigil, Duffy got to whisper, "Gotcha." He hurried into the building's lobby and called the precinct. He then called Humph. They met up at a hotel on Seventh Avenue. Hotel staff directed them to the eleventh floor. To avoid noise complaints, that floor and the ones above and below had been rented by what turned out to be a clique of musically inclined Nazi lovers.

The cops had no trouble finding the party room. They could hear laughter over the sound of drums, a clarinet and a piano, then singing.

The door was unlocked. The cops entered and found themselves no more than ten feet from the banker-singer.

"Get out of here," he said. "You have no business here."

The police pushed their way into the room.

"Do you know who I am?" exclaimed the investment banker.

The sergeant turned to him, and with his face inches from the money man's, said:

"Well, sir, with that get-up of yours, it's kinda hard to tell who, or what, you are." Some of his men chuckled in agreement.

The police took the names of the other partygoers. However, they pulled out handcuffs for the investment banker. When it sunk in that he was being arrested, he begged the cops for permission to remove his makeup before going to the precinct.

"This is a very busy Saturday night," said the sergeant. "No time for that."

He was told he was being charged with disturbing the peace. When he got to the station, he was met by Detective Higgins. To prevent the man from posting bail, he was charged with suspected treasonous activity.

The interrogation lasted well into the night. The man was silver-tongued. However, after circuitous questions, demands for clarification and needless reviews of his statement so far, the man was wearing down.

"Your makeup is running, sir," Humph told him. "Want a tissue or two?"

With the prisoner evidently on his last legs, Higgins stood up and laid it on the line.

"We know as a fact that you arrange investments by Americans in shell companies, which you use to disguise the true ownership of the investments. These companies set up in neutral countries to avoid detection. Switzerland and Sweden are favorite places for these shell companies." The banker stared at Higgins but said nothing.

Higgins paused to ask a young constable to bring him a cup of tea. While waiting for it, Higgins resumed.

"We also know, sir, that traitors like you can invest through intermediaries or foreign banks, ones that turn a blind eye to the source of the funds. Shall I go on?"

The tea arrived. The banker asked for a cup.

"No talkee, no tea, sir," said Higgins.

Humph was greatly enjoying his friend's interrogation technique.

The sun was coming up. The banker's sleeves now bore most of his facial makeup. His face was nightmarish.

At last, he started to talk.

He claimed that all he was guilty of was investing in American companies that "may have" had operations in Germany.

"Are we talking about inconsequential companies?"

"Not exactly," said the banker.

"Let me name a few," said Higgins. "Pray tell, how inconsequential are the following? General Motors, IT&T, Eastman Kodak, Standard Oil, Coca-Cola, Westinghouse?"

The banker nodded what was clearly a weary head. Unlike Higgins and the others, he had been drinking for hours before his arrest.

"Yes, I invested client money in those companies over the years."

Higgins quickly corrected him.

"No, you invested your clients' money in them only when it looked like Germany was going to fully rearm and attack Europe. While you were being escorted here, sir, my men were executing a search warrant on your offices. I expect that at this very moment, they have discovered evidence to support every charge I'm leveling against you."

Higgins sat and made a point of enjoying his tea to the maximum. Moments after the banker's had tea arrived, nearly cold, Humph stood again to list other ways Wall Street was effectively investing in the Nazi war effort.

"They—you—invest in German subsidiaries of American companies." He named Ford Werek, a subsidiary of Ford Motor Company. "And, oh yes, we can't forget General Motors and its Opel division. You certainly had a rich selection of potential investment targets."

The banker shrugged his shoulders.

"And, may I mention that there's a black mark for moving funds all over the world and making investments untraceable? My late dear mother always told me that instead of deciding on a career as a copper, I should have chosen investment banking."

By the time the banker was taken to a cell, and Humph, Duffy and Higgins had returned to his office, it was 8:33 a.m.

"A long night," said Higgins, "but I for one am not the least bit pooped. What say we escape to the bar next door?" He got no argument.

"It's on me, boys."

When the second round appeared on the table—neither Humph nor Duffy had seen Higgins order it—Higgins grabbed his new glass and raised it in a toast.

"Can't say how grateful I am to the two of you. And I'd like to add a footnote to this toast. You, Humph, I know you were hurt that the Army rejected you, but of late you have been mowing down Nazi supporters as if you had a military-issue machine gun. You simply couldn't have been more effective overseas than you are here in America. Proud to know you."

It was noon before Humph dragged himself home. Rebecca had Sunday off. Thank God, thought Humph. She took him straight to bed, where, eyes closed, he proceeded to ramble about the takedown of a traitorous Wall Street investment banker. He didn't mention the praise from Higgins, but he wanted to. When his words started to trail off, Rebecca gave him a kiss. "Well done, soldier."

CHAPTER 25

WHEN Humph roused himself the next day after a fourteen-hour sleep, he walked into the front room to find Eve there but no Christa. Rebecca had stayed home for some reason.

Humph went to the kitchen for coffee. Rebecca followed him.

"As you know, Eve adopted Christa, but although she seemed happy at first, she's clearly got issues," Rebecca said, speaking in a lowered voice.

"She's met a boy, an older boy, mid-twenties. Eve has never met him. Long story short, Christa insists she wants to move in with him. Eve says she and the girl are fighting all the time. Eve's dream of being a mother has fallen flat on its face. She has no idea what to do."

Humph let out an enormous sigh as he sat on a kitchen chair. Though he was only half awake, his first thought was whether he was crazy wanting children of his own.

Rebecca took one of his hands in hers, sitting down next to him.

"Humph, do you think you could try to find out what you can about this boy? You have no new cases, right?"

That was true, Humph said. Besides, he was never good at handling downtime. Using the kitchen table, he pushed himself to his feet and went to the living room with Rebecca. He sat beside Eve.

"So sorry, Eve. Can't imagine how tough this is. I know you felt she was your daughter, which, now legally, thanks to you, she is."

After a long silence, Rebecca broke in.

"Worst case, Eve, even if Christa goes with this guy, it doesn't mean she's lost to you. Listen, when I was a teenager, I ran away from home twice. And my parents were always loving."

Eve was clearly relieved by Rebecca's words.

Rebecca seized on the change in mood to suggest that Humph might be able to find out a thing or two about the boy Christa was so attracted to. "Would you like him to try?"

Eve thought about it for a strangely long time. Having grown up without a mother, there was no one more independent than Eve. She'd been fighting since her teens to stand alone and stand strong.

At last, Eve rose and, with one knee on the sofa, leaned over Humph. She kissed him on the forehead. Still gently holding his head, she pulled her face back and said, "Yes. Please, papa."

After sitting back down, Eve said she didn't even know the boy's address.

"You'll have to follow Christa the next time she goes out. At least she's good about telling me when she's going out."

"OK," said Humph. "That works. I'm off for a few days, so just call me and I'll try to get to your place in time to follow her."

The first couple of times, he arrived too late. But it seemed there was a pattern for Christa's visits to her boyfriend. It was always on a weekend, which suggested the young man had a job, maybe even an evening or night job.

Humph phoned Duffy to ask if he could get him a car he could park near Eve's place and use it to sleep in while he waited for the girl to step out.

"You'll have one shortly, my friend." Then he added, "Not quite the same as surveilling a Nazi-loving traitor, is it?"

The following weekend, Humph trailed Christa to a rooming house not far from Duffy's place. Christa stayed there for three hours, then left. She took a taxi home.

"Where," wondered Humph, "did that money come from? Does the boyfriend have a good job?"

Once he made sure Christa got home, he went home and phoned Duffy. It occurred to him that since Duffy lived close by, he might not mind going to the boyfriend's door to conduct a neighborhood survey of sorts. Hopefully, his survey would show whether the boy was gainfully employed in some way. Being a Bowery lad himself, Duffy might be able to get the boyfriend chatting. "It's worth a shot, Duff."

Duff showed up at Humph's door two weeks later.

"If you want to hear my report, you'll have to pour me one of your best."

Humph couldn't argue. However, he was too anxious to hear the results to pour a drink for himself.

"OK, Duff, out with it."

Duff savored his first sip for an annoyingly long time.

"Duff!"

"Hold your horses, big guy. Hold your horses.

"It turns out that the young man in question is, first of all, an affable sort. Secondly, his main employment is that of a barrel-maker. It's actually more remunerative than you'd think. It's a dying skill, and it's not the kind of job that attracts lads raised on Hollywood dreams at the local cinema. However, it pains me to report that, like almost every other lad on the Lower East Side, he profits from sideline scams. It's in the blood, I guess. I often even wonder whether you, as a Lower East Sider born and bred, aren't running a few yourself."

"These scams, Duff, do they involve anything that could land him in jail for a long time?"

"I doubt it, but perhaps if he's serious about Eve's daughter and wants to keep her, you might want to throw the fear of God into him. He's a little guy, five-two maybe. With the likes of you looming over him, he might very well be accommodating to your desires."

Two days later, Humph gave Eve the gist of Duffy's report. No stranger herself to minor deviations to the law, she was not alarmed at the young man's occasional forays into theft in one form or another. But, yes, they would have to stop, as Humph recommended.

Eve was relieved. The guy wasn't a murderer or rapist or employed by the Mob.

She told Humph she'd have a long talk with Christa.

"I'll try to make her understand that, first of all, I get her need to feel like an adult and make her own decisions, and second, that I've learned—I won't say how—that her guy is straight, except for a couple of things. I'll ask that she tell him that unless he foregoes those hobbies, he's not in her life."

She added: "I've been there, Dad. I can make her understand."

Humph wished her good luck and returned home, energized by having had a mini mystery to solve.

Within twenty-four hours, he was grumpy beyond measure. Was he going to spend the rest of his life waiting for the phone to ring or a case to miraculously fall in his lap?

CHAPTER 26

"COME in."

The message was a telegram. It arrived at 5:42 a.m. It was signed "Higgins".

Considering the hour, it was obviously urgent. He looked out the window and, to his surprise, a police car was already outside.

Humph threw on a shirt and rushed out the door, only to notice, as he found himself under a streetlamp, that he was still wearing his pajama bottoms. He was still groggy enough to consider continuing without them, but just before getting in the patrol car, he realized he had no idea whom he might encounter at the police station.

The cop behind the wheel had little to say when Humph asked how he was doing. He wasn't insulted. The guy had been on duty all night, and his shift was almost over. It had been a boring one. Since the curfew was imposed, the streets were eerily dark at night. That made it almost impossible to spot suspicious characters lurking about. Few law-abiding citizens went for a night-time stroll either. The reports of muggings had declined sharply. On the other hand, life had become better for burglars. The arrest quota system had become pointless, which made life easier for the guys pounding beats. However, without that pressure to make a certain number of arrests, the patrolling cops found the nights longer.

When Humph arrived at the Mott Street precinct station, he was led to the second floor and invited to sit down. Higgins wasn't there. He showed up twenty minutes later, long enough for Humph to realize he was still tired.

With Higgins was a tall, skinny man, about Humph's age. Higgins sat and the stranger passed him a paper.

"I apologize for the early summons," Higgins said. "With me is OSS Agent Marty McLoud who has an early morning flight to catch. In fact, he returned from Buenos Aires only three days ago. It's not the most relaxing journey. Not having time to enjoy the comforts of a sea voyage, Marty had to fly. Just this year, Pan Am has created the first routes connecting North and South America. However, while you can fly from here to Miami, once you get there, you take a tiresome series of connecting flights through Central America and down the east coast of South America to Buenos Aires. If you ask me," Higgins added, "Marty deserves a medal."

Humph raised his hand.

"Detective Higgins, may I offer to spare Marty the agony of the return journey by volunteering to go in his place?" Several of the other detectives and officers in the room chuckled. Everyone knew the destination was an exotic one.

"Your kindness is only exceeded by your tenacity," said Higgins, smiling. "I remember you recently stating that you would love to take your lovely wife to Argentina." Humph acknowledged the recollection with a slight bow of his head.

"Down to business," said Higgins. "I invited you because you're all familiar with the art forging case of last year, the one involving the Met. We never caught the mastermind, the forger who made it all possible. Until very recently, we thought he was still hiding out in England. That turns out to be inaccurate. He has shown up in Argentina several times.

"We know that thanks to Marty and the OSS. I'll give you some background."

He explained that earlier in the year, the NYPD had nabbed a handful of New York gallery owners who were trying to smuggle valuable art to a filthy rich Argentinian, Nazi-loving art collector. They revealed that their scheme bore similarities with the Met theft. The artwork they were hoping to send south to the collector would be meddled with by a forger, none other than Benjamin Borasco, the one that got away from them.

"According to the fellas we nabbed a while back," said Higgins, "the works they tried to send to Argentina, to the rich collector, were then to be put in the hands of Mr. Borasco. Borasco would then forge documents such as provenance records, certificates of authenticity and so on to deceive potential buyers about the true origin and value of a stolen piece of art. Once that was done, theoretically at least, the paintings would be sold internationally at greatly inflated prices. The mark-up would then be shared by Borasco, the collector and our thieving gallery owners here in New York. That money would be added to what the gallery owners recuperated from their insurance companies, to whom they'd reported the artwork as being stolen."

Marty then stood and stated simply that on his previous trip to Buenos Aires, he had cornered the collector.

"Using the information provided to Detective Higgins and myself, thanks in large part to Humph, I cornered the collector at his home in the midst of a cocktail party that looked like a Hollywood gathering of stars in glitzy gowns and men in dashing black ties and an excess of Brylcreem."

He said he and a local agent from the Argentinian equivalent of the OSS, the *Servicio de Informaciones del Estado* (SIE), which, Marty said, translated to the State Information Service, had confronted the collector and politely suggested they retire to a less public area of the mansion.

"As usual in such cases, the rich guy pleaded ignorance when we first questioned him. Stage two began when we pressed harder and in return got not denials but warnings that he personally knew government and police officials of the highest rank. He even dared say to me, 'I'll have you thrown out of the country.'"

After a good hour of questioning, Marty said, there were repeated knocks on the door from party guests begging the collector to rejoin the party.

"Our collector was starting to fidget. It was then that I asked him when he last saw Señor Borasco."

The collector blurted out: "Not for ages. I barely know the man. I can't even remember why he contacted me."

"His impatience to get rid of us compelled him to reveal that he clearly knew the forger. At that point, we took him to SIE headquarters for more intensive questioning in the hope that the grim surroundings would make it clear that resistance was futile. We ended up learning that he had employed Borasco on several occasions, which, he admitted, had been highly profitable. He volunteered that Borasco shared his pro-Nazi beliefs, and finally, that Borasco had moved back to England. He had his address, which he used to send telegrams to the forger."

Marty said they left the collector in a cell until morning. In the meantime, they returned to his mansion and went straight to his office. They confiscated every piece of paper they could find linking him with deals with the forger, letters from other Nazi supporters in the Argentinian government and letters to people he knew in Germany.

"His goose was cooked better than a fine Argentinian steak."

Laughter followed. Higgins told him that he'd never heard a better mixed metaphor about food.

He then thanked the OSS agent and offered a patrol car to take him to the airport.

After he had left, Higgins asked Humph to remain behind.

Humph's day had started earlier than usual because of the summons from Higgins.

"Do you think it's too early to continue at our drinking hole?"

"Yes," said Higgins without bothering to look at his watch. "This won't take long."

Higgins said the British were still willing to extradite the forger.

"Of course, we have to find him first and arrest him. Understandably, with the war and all, their policing resources are stretched to the limit. We've been losing men to the armed forces but nowhere near as many as they have in England."

"That is quite understandable," Humph said. His heart started to beat faster as he waited for Higgins to continue.

"Coffee, tea?" the detective asked.

Humph wondered whether his friend was dragging out the conversation on purpose. Higgins's eyes never revealed anything.

"Neither," said Humph.

Higgins got himself a cup of tea on the other side of the room and returned to his desk, walking slowly, apparently not risking spilling his precious tea.

"Ordinarily," said Higgins at last, "we would send one of our men to England to escort the wanted man back to

New York. But the blasted war complicates things. We can't get there by sea. It's far too likely that a kraut U-boat would end the voyage prematurely. And you may or may not know that there are no commercial flights to England."

"Damn it. I need a drink," said Humph. "You seem intent on dragging this out all afternoon."

Finally, Higgins gave a tiny smile.

"You win, Humph. To the pub we go."

Before leaving, Higgins said he had to speak to a couple of detectives about other matters. Humph was tempted to close his eyes and drop off to sleep.

He did, but a slap on the back told him Higgins was finally ready to head to the flatfoot oasis.

Not a word was spoken until each of them had taken a sip of their drinks, beer for the detective and Scotch for the private eye.

"As I said," Higgins resumed, "getting to Merry Old isn't so easy anymore. I would, if you're willing, like to send you to arrest and return Borasco to our shores. You know as much about him as anybody."

Humph needed a few minutes to take in the idea. Before replying, he ordered another drink. Higgins declined.

"Of course," said Humph. "I'd give my right arm to go."

"You know you'd be at great risk just being in England. The Luftwaffe is bombing the bejesus out of cities across the country. They're turning London into a pile of rubble. What will Rebecca think of you going?"

Humph hadn't thought of that.

"I guess she won't like it, but she knows risk is part of my job. And she hates Borasco for what he did to the young Argentinian painter. He's a friend of the family now."

"And your Spanish teacher, yes?"

Humph nodded with a smile.

"So, Higgins, how do I get there?"

Higgins replied that he'd already talked to the OSS about that.

"As you know, we're sending military supplies to England. They include planes, notably B-17 bombers. Apparently, they're a technical marvel. You would fly in one of them."

The idea excited Humph and it showed on his face.

"But there's a catch," said Higgins. "The journey will be long, tedious in the extreme and uncomfortable as hell."

He explained that it wasn't a direct route.

The Air Force, he said, used a series of intermediate stops known as the North Atlantic air ferry route. It included stops in Newfoundland, Labrador, Greenland and Iceland before reaching England. They did this to avoid Germans. The journey would take up to eight days.

"So?" said Humph. "A ship takes that long."

"But a ship is comfortable. You get a comfortable bed. There's a bar. Good food."

"What are you getting at?" Humph said.

"Simply put, Humph, you will hate military planes by the time you land in England. God knows how you'll raise your spirits enough to face up to your return journey. You'll probably have to ingest a dose or two of the famous British stiff upper lip."

Humph tried to imagine the flight but couldn't. He'd never been in a plane.

"Why don't the Brits find and arrest Borasco? You say they know where he might be. One of their men could bring him to our shores."

Higgins said the idea was brought up at his meeting with the OSS agent.

"The answer, Humph, was that the British cops can't spare anyone to do that. Besides, as they pointed out, Borasco is our man of the hour, not theirs."

Humph went silent, which pleased Higgins because it meant he had probably accepted the mission and was trying to picture what he might need and what he should be prepared for.

"What about papers? Papers that would get me into the country."

Instantly, Higgins replied.

"Thought of that already. I can no longer send you as an NYPD cop, but the OSS will issue papers saying you represent them. They will also describe you as a former NYPD officer. We added that to reassure British cops that you know what you're doing."

"When?" asked Humph.

"Soon," said Higgins, "but I don't know exactly when. I expect we'll be given short notice about the next shipment of bombers."

Humph went home and waited for Rebecca to get there.

Before she arrived, Higgins called.

"October fourth. You'll be picked up and taken to the airport at 7 a.m. Be sure to pack, especially warm clothes."

The weather in New York was still pleasant, the temperature well into the seventies most days. He never would have thought of bringing winter clothes.

Rebecca didn't arrive until after seven. Humph was asleep on the sofa.

She changed from her work clothes, made her man a sandwich and sat beside him. She woke him with a soft voice.

He pulled her next to him, holding on until he was awake enough to speak.

"I'm going on a trip."

Rebecca waited for the rest.

"I'm going after Borasco. That means I'm going to England."

"When?"

"Next week, Sunday, the fourth."

"That's exciting, Humph. Finally, we get the bastard."

Humph held up his hand to say, "Slow down."

"We're only guessing where he's hiding. And I'm not sure how much help I'll be getting from Scotland Yard. I don't know how long I'll be gone."

Rebecca suddenly felt a chill. She put her arm around him and led him to bed. Humph willingly turned his back on thoughts about his immediate future.

CHAPTER 27

A jeep arrived in Tompkins Square at precisely 7 a.m.

"Good morning, sir," said the driver, taking Humph's luggage from him.

"A good day for flying, sir."

It was and Humph felt less anxious already.

Twenty minutes later, Humph questioned the driver.

"Hey, LaGuardia Field is that way."

"That's not our destination, sir. We're going to Long Island, a military field."

Getting no response from Humph, he added, "You might know it as Floyd Bennett Field. When the war started, it became part of Naval Air Station New York. The Coast Guard also uses it. Besides being a departure point for shipping military supplies overseas, this is the center of our defense of New York City."

"I understand," said Humph, who was now wondering what other surprises might be in store.

He didn't have to wait long. The jeep took him directly to the bomber that would take him to England. An officer of some kind welcomed him.

"Let me introduce you to the craft. It will take some getting used to. But first, please show me your papers."

Humph complied, all the while never taking his eyes off the flying beast before him.

When he finally got aboard, he had to duck. The interior wasn't built for men his size.

"To your left, sir, is the cockpit," the officer said. "Take a peek, if you wish."

Like the rest of the aircraft, it was cramped, with an impossibly large assortment of controls and gauges. At least, thought Humph, the pilot and co-pilot could enjoy a panoramic view of the world outside. The same couldn't be said of the rest of the interior.

The word "cramped" didn't do it justice, thought Humph. It was sinking in that this would be his home for the next seven or eight days.

The officer pointed out the bombardier's compartment, located in the nose.

"It contains controls for dropping bombs. The bombardier also operates the nose guns."

He then pointed out the navigator's station, the radio room in the mid-section of the plane, which also had a machine gun, and then the bomb bay in the center of the aircraft. There were narrow catwalks allowing the crew to move about as necessary. The tour ended with the waist gunners' positions and that of the tail gunner.

The officer then said he felt duty-bound to mention that not only was the plane cramped, but it would also be noisy to the point of being deafening. It would also be cold. The plane was unpressurized and temperatures could plunge drastically. He told Humph that at those altitudes, oxygen masks were necessary.

Humph didn't need to hear the officer's last bit of description. He'd seen for himself that there were no seats for most crew members. "They often stand or crouch at their stations for hours." Humph's mind jumped to memories of the luxurious voyage he took to Cuba with Rebecca.

"Not to worry too much, sir. We've jerry-rigged a chair for you not too far behind the cockpit, which gives you a glimpse of the sky. It's not much, but it helps if you suffer from claustrophobia."

The officer went forward and turned, pointing out Humph's chair. Humph was suddenly depressed. He dropped into the chair and asked:

"When do we leave? I want to get this over with."

Forty minutes later, he was air bound, headed for Newfoundland.

Each stop in the leap-frog journey was a chance to stretch his legs, eat and carry on conversations with the crew and base staff. His first-ever flight was rapidly extinguishing what had once been a dream. He decided he was quite happy with his feet on the ground. How the Air Force did this day in and day out, he had no idea. They all deserved medals.

The next stop at Reykjavik was a disappointment. He always pictured Iceland as being under eternal snow. It was on the barren side but green, nonetheless.

On the eighth day, a crew member took him by the elbow and led him closer to the cockpit and its windows. Below was Ireland, the crewman yelled in his ear. Humph could only return a thumbs-up. What a beautiful sight, he thought. "So," he said to himself, "that's the land that pushed Duffy into the world."

The final descent brought with it a disappointing view of Heathrow Airport. What he saw was an airport not unlike the William Bennet Field in New York. It was only after they'd landed and the noise stopped that he was told they'd arrived at RAF Bovingdon in Dorset. Bovingdon was being used by U.S. forces during the arms buildup in England.

Humph was met once again by a jeep.

"Off to London, sir?"

"Can't wait," said Humph with a smile. "That flight was about all I could stomach."

The driver chuckled.

"Won't take long, sir. It's less than thirty miles from the city."

On the way, Humph learned that the airport at Bovingdon had the advantage of being at slightly higher elevation than Heathrow.

"When London's hidden under a peasouper, the skies over Bovingdon are usually clear," the driver said.

As requested in the OSS instructions, a humble hotel had a reservation for Humph. It was located not far from Scotland Yard, which would be his destination the next day after what he hoped would be a good and peaceful night's rest. Humph allowed a bellhop to take his luggage upstairs to the room. A man used to walking great distances, a week of being absolutely sedentary had left him exhausted. Thank God for elevators, he thought, as he stepped out onto his floor.

He asked the bellhop, already waiting in his room, where he could eat nearby.

"Fancy fish and chips, sir? If you do, I can personally recommend a place two doors down."

Humph gave him a better tip than he would normally. He was famished.

"The fish and chips are better here," he said to himself as he returned to his room. Partially restored by the meal, he was able to walk up the one flight of stairs to his room. He ran a bath, his first since leaving New York. He made it last, coming close to dozing off in the tub. He then went straight to bed and straight to sleep.

Just before midnight, he awoke. Air raid sirens wailed. Minutes later, the far-off drone of aircraft engines became a roar as German bombers filled the skies above the city. Humph swore the hotel itself was shaking as bombs landed time and time again. Part of the rumble he heard turned out to be buildings collapsing into the streets. The staccato bursts of anti-aircraft guns echoed across the city. The sky brightened as flames rose to the sky.

Humph had read about the devastating Blitz in the New York papers. Even with his fertile imagination, he knew now that the accounts failed to transmit the horror the English were enduring night after night.

Suddenly, the roar of the bombers disappeared. From his hotel window, he could see the smoke and the flames. He couldn't bear to go down to the street. Firefighters and ambulances were everywhere. Humph learned afterward that the night's attack sent thousands to shelter in the subway tunnels. Why had no one in the hotel banged on his door, telling him to flee to the streets? It was a question he didn't dare ask when morning came. He was one of the lucky ones. He had escaped unharmed.

He'd had his baptism of fire. He made his way to Scotland Yard with one thought in his mind. It was time to put the cuffs on a man who was doing everything he could to provide money to Hitler through forged art.

An inspector was expecting his visit. Humph gladly accepted tea and biscuits in his office.

"Quite a welcome," the inspector said, referring to the German raid.

"How you stay sane while enduring this I'll never know," said Humph. "So much more terrifying than I had imagined."

"It's astonishing what one can get accustomed to. Of course, you never, hopefully, get accustomed to death, but as for the rest of this bad play, you can. That's the only way to stay sane. You may already have read that we've sent the children out of the city, away from the bombs. One hopes they'll see their parents again someday when this is over."

The inspector sat upright in his chair and suggested they get down to business.

"You know where Borasco is?" Humph asked.

"Yes and no. We're sure we spotted him a month back entering a house outside the city, in a hamlet full of cozy, rather old cottages and little else. The kind of place you have to live for a few decades before anyone ventures to bid you good morning."

The following morning, two constables and another inspector drove Humph to the village where they hoped to find the forger.

Only one or two people appeared in the main street. It was so quiet that Humph wondered whether the chirping of birds constituted disturbing the peace.

But the village was quaint and so far removed from the thunderous horrors that Londoners lived with.

While Humph and the inspector remained in the car, the two constables entered the one and only pub. They were armed with an artist's depiction of the man they were searching for.

They returned to happily state that their man appeared in town now and then for supplies.

The inspector told the constables to ask the people who operated stores selling fish, meat, vegetables and pantry goods, and perhaps the chemist's shop.

"Chemist?" asked Humph.

"I believe you call them drug stores," said the inspector.

As the constables walked away, the inspector suggested that he and Humph take in the sun while sitting on a bench a few yards away.

Half an hour later, the constables returned. They reported that two or three shopkeepers said the face was familiar. They suggested they return on market day.

"Makes sense," said the inspector. "Let's do that."

With that, they returned to the city.

When they got back to Scotland Yard, Humph decided to stretch his legs and walk to the Parliament Buildings. However, it was much closer to the Yard than he'd expected. He kept walking until he found a pub. He made straight for the bar and accepted a pint of the beer on tap. Patrons played darts. The scene was straight from novels he'd read. Apart from not being cold, the beer settled in his stomach as satisfyingly as a meal. An hour later, Humph headed back to the hotel. He felt a sense of well-being, which he couldn't figure out.

That night, there was no bombing raid.

Two days later, Humph and the Yard cops returned to the hamlet early in the morning. The market was already open when they arrived. That day, the constables were in plain clothes. They immediately began meandering through the stalls. Morning turned to afternoon and, after getting the inspector's permission, one of the constables took a pub break. That whole time, Humph knew he had to stay hidden. Borasco likely knew him from New York when Humph was doing surveillance work.

Just before 4 p.m., the constables returned together.

"We spotted him, sir," they said. "Get out and look this way," he said. "The skinny guy there, about twenty-five yards ahead, with a green hat and a bag over his shoulder."

The inspector told them to get in the car. Slowly, they moved in the direction of the forger.

"Let him get home. I want to nail him there. We might find evidence in the house."

It turned out that the forger lived not far, a walkable distance even with a load of supplies.

Once he had reached an open road, which was not much wider than a country lane, the inspector told the driver to hold back. "Give him several minutes, then advance until he's in sight again."

The cottages had become far apart. There was little danger of losing sight of Borasco.

Finally, they saw Borasco turn onto a short walkway leading to a small house. The constables got out of the car and approached it on foot, waiting for Borasco to enter before getting within a few feet of the door. They waved toward the car, indicating that the inspector and the American should follow them.

When they caught up with the constables, Humph used hand signals to indicate that one of the constables should check for a side or back entrance. A minute later, the inspector knocked on the door.

"Police, Mr. Borasco. We need a minute of your time."

They heard a noise from within the house, but Borasco had not come to the door. Humph nudged the inspector aside and threw his bulk against the door. It popped open so easily that Humph almost fell to the floor.

One of the constables rushed Borasco. He was holding a gun to his head. Humph bellowed.

"Disarm the bastard! Now! I want him alive!"

The constable didn't reach for the gun. Instead, he tackled him like the rugby player he was on weekends, churning his legs as he gripped the man behind his knees. The gun flew from Borasco's hands as he hit the floor. The inspector pounced on it.

On the drive back to London, with Borasco squished between the two constables in the back seat, the inspector said that Humph needed to wear "that bloody grin" all the way. "We share your joy."

From Scotland Yard, Humph phoned his Air Force liaison.

"We got our man, sergeant. Wheels up whenever you're ready."

Two Scotland Yard constables drove Humph and his prisoner to RAF Bovingdon for the flight home.

Strange how the mind works, thought Humph. Instead of rejoicing in his success, he found himself thinking that the seat in the police car was the last comfort he would experience until arriving in the United States a week from now.

Upon boarding the bomber, Humph saw that the Air Force had authorized a second seat to be installed, next to his. Humph let three Air Force officers watch over Borasco, bound hand and foot, while he hurried to the base headquarters to send a message to Higgins.

"Military mission accomplished. War criminal aboard returning Flying Fortress. Tell Rebecca."

CHAPTER 28

WHEN Humph reached his door in Tompkins Square, Duffy beat him to the punch opening it.

"A war hero returns," he bellowed.

Rebecca rushed into his arms. She smothered him with kisses. Then she dragged him to the middle of the living room. Humph, weary to the point of dizziness from the interminable return flight, spotted Higgins and a couple of other cops of long acquaintance, then his eyes landed on Eve and Christa. Duffy then barged his way between Rebecca and Humph and thrust a pitcher-sized glass of Scotch into Humph's hands.

The next morning, Rebecca let Humph sleep in. When he opened his eyes, he barely remembered any details of the evening except for falling into a sea of happiness.

Rebecca told him that Higgins would appreciate a call when he felt up to it.

First, Humph and Rebecca went to their local diner for breakfast, a good American breakfast. Humph was ridiculously picky about the way home fries were made.

Rebecca caught him on Eve's situation.

"Christa told her boyfriend that they weren't to be. Apparently, she decided she wasn't ready for the outside world. She reasoned that at eighteen, she was perhaps too young to know much about it. And after her rape and brainwashing by her father, she needed time. Eve told her "baby steps". Christa told her she'd nailed it in those two words. Needless to say, Eve is on cloud nine. She's got her girl back."

Humph asked what Higgins had to say, if anything.

"He said he would never tell you this in person, but in his opinion, you have served this country's war effort as effectively, and courageously, as any soldier. We all drank to that. In fact, we drank copious amounts to that. My head hurts."

"And Duff?"

"Well, he was happy when you told him you'd seen his homeland from the air and marveled at how green it really was. I think he liked the fact that you thought of him in your discomfort so high in the sky."

It was two days before Humph showed up at the precinct. He'd walked all the way from home and felt all the better for it. He had no appointment with Higgins, but he knew that if the detective was in the building, he'd see him.

His wait turned out to be only five minutes. Higgins offered a handshake and a firm embrace.

"You did us proud," he said. "Coffee, tea or Scotch?"

"Nothing," said Humph. "I'm happy being me this morning.

Higgins then said they'd already interrogated the forger.

"He revealed lots of details we needed to close last year's case and ones that will let us bump up the charges against this year's pack of art gallery owners who tried to smuggle art to Argentina. Two cases closed in two interviews. Not bad, and it's thanks to you, Humph."

Higgins then asked if Humph wanted a go at Borasco before they turned him over to the prosecutor.

"I'll have to think about that," Humph replied. "If you had asked me a month ago, I would have said yes, but now I feel totally distanced from the case. It's like my mind is tired and fed up with Borasco. He's in good hands, Higgins, namely yours. I'd like to say goodbye to it all."

After a moment, he added:

"I don't know. Maybe I'm just tired from freezing to death in a B-17."

Higgins said he understood completely. He then added:

"I called you in this morning not to talk about the case. I just wanted to say you could see Borasco if you wanted.

"The real reason I wanted to see you is that I've been talking to the OSS again. They're delighted, as I am, that you succeeded on your mission for them and that you did it in record time. And the fact you brought the suspect home alive was an added bonus. The OSS, thanks to you, now knows that Nazi supporters with money abound in this country. Bringing them to justice will make an important contribution to the war effort. I made sure they understood that you have been corralling these traitors since before we entered the war, since before we knew they were enemies of America."

Humph thanked Higgins.

"I'm not finished, Humph."

"I asked you here to tell you that the OSS has contacted the White House. They think you deserve recognition not just for your recent success in England, but for your earlier efforts on behalf of this nation. The president wants to award you a medal."

Humph was dumbfounded.

"You're joking, you Scottish scoundrel."

"Not in the slightest." He tossed Humph a letter.

It was from the Office of the President of the United States.

It read:

"The Congressional Gold Medal. It is an award bestowed by the United States Congress. It is Congress's highest expression of national appreciation for distinguished achievements and contributions by individuals, institutions or groups. It can be awarded to anyone Congress deems worthy."

Higgins gave Humph time to let the news sink in.

"You're worthy, in spades, Humph. Congratulations. Your war has been a success."

Humph was speechless. He slowly made his way back home.

Rebecca was at work when he arrived. He wasn't ready to think of what all this meant to his life. He phoned Duffy.

"I think I need to get drunk, my friend."

"Happy to oblige a man in need," said Duffy.

"Can you get a car and pick me up?"

Duffy arrived half an hour later. He knocked on Humph's door then retreated to the car. He held open the door to the passenger's side.

"Where to, sir?" Duffy said, pretending to be a servant.

"The Bronx," said Humph, much to Duffy's surprise. Humph had said many a time that nothing good, including women, had ever come from the Bronx. The remark was always a dig at Duffy who seemed to be an irresistible attraction for women of the borough.

Duffy led him to a bar that couldn't have been darker. Duffy himself went to the bar and returned with doubles, one Scottish whisky, the other Irish. They drank in silence.

When Humph finished his drink, he declared that this was not a hunt for women. Even in the darkness, it was clear that Duffy was crestfallen.

"No, sir," said Humph. "All I seek is a return to reality. I want to investigate a cheating husband. I want to expose a Mob-directed extortion of a municipal employee. I want to rescue a damsel in distress at a brothel. I want New York to be New York again. I don't want to have to think about the welfare of the rest of the world."

"You don't want much, do you, laddie?"

Duffy dragged him out of the bar, shoved him into the car and headed for another club. A strip club.

"Maybe this place will give you some good old New York reality."

It didn't work.

"Take me home, Duff. Please."

Over breakfast the next morning, Humph placed the Congressional letter on the table in front of Rebecca.

Rebecca thought Humph, though uncommunicative, was surprisingly sober after a night with Duffy, but she decided not to pry. The evening was clearly something Humph needed.

As if in a trance, Humph asked:

"Did we ever sail to Puerto Rico?"

"You know damn well we didn't."

"Thought so," said Humph.

Rebecca waited and waited.

Finally, Humph said he'd have to check, but it was probably not safe to sail there.

"Why would the Germans give a damn about Puerto Rico?"

"They're targeting every shipping route used to send arms or supplies to the Allies. They're damn good at it."

"Would you like to chance it?"

"You're out of your mind, Humph."

"Pass the salt, please," he answered.

Almost a month later, he and Rebecca traveled by train to Washington. There, Humph expressed his dislike of wearing a monkey suit for the medal ceremony. "Shush!" she told him, straightening his black tie.

THE END

ABOUT THE AUTHOR

Wayne Clark is a Montreal writer and author
of six other New York-based novels, including the
international award-winning literary fiction novel
he & She. In addition to writing fiction he has
worked as a journalist, copywriter and translator.